THREE SUMMERS

To: Claire

I hope you enjoy the Book!

R. N. Maynard

THREE SUMMERS

THE GREATEST GAME

DN Maynard

TATE PUBLISHING
AND ENTERPRISES, LLC

Published by Tate Publishing & Enterprises, LLC
127 E. Trade Center Terrace | Mustang, Oklahoma 73064 USA
1.888.361.9473 | www.tatepublishing.com

Tate Publishing is committed to excellence in the publishing industry. The company reflects the philosophy established by the founders, based on Psalm 68:11,

"The Lord gave the word and great was the company of those who published it."

Book design copyright © 2016 by Tate Publishing, LLC. All rights reserved.
Cover design by Samson Lim
Interior design by Manolito Bastasa

Published in the United States of America

ISBN: 978-1-68333-488-0
1. Fiction / Historical
2. Fiction / Christian / Historical
16.05.03

— Introduction —

LIFE IS A series of breaths, a series of steps, a series of firsts, a series of lasts. Life is a series of opportunities, a series of challenges, a series of shouts, a series of quiet moments, a series of births, a series of deaths. Life is a series of dreams, a series of memories, a series of games, a series of summers.

Our lives begin as a blank canvas, and as our lives unfold, the joys, sorrows, and personal experiences we have shape the colors we paint on our canvas. Our canvas is made up of hundreds of individual threads interwoven together; if we were to pull out a single thread and examine it, we would find different colors spread across it. This story is about one thread and the colors found on it.

— Prologue —

I T WAS MEMORIAL Day weekend. I remember, because there were only seven more days of school, and we always camped as a family over the holiday weekend.

My nuclear family consisted of my parents, my three sisters, and myself. I was the oldest child, thank God. Being the only boy with three sisters was sometimes lonely, but spending time camping on holidays with my extended family helped to make it bearable. Traditions are important in my family, and Memorial Day weekends meant camping in our secret place, an almost magical place, on an island in the middle of the Lewis River.

In the middle of the island, there's a grove of old-growth trees so dense, they form a canopy impenetrable by direct sunlight or rain. Beneath the canopy, decades of fallen fir needles and cedar bows cover the ground so thick, it feels like you're walking on a box-spring mattress when you enter this magical kingdom.

Our campsite encompassed five geographical areas. The center area contained the meeting area, a place of relaxation, conversation, and meditation. It consisted of a large fire pit surrounded by folding chairs, a dozen or so picnic tables, two cast iron stoves for preparing meals, and an old Coke pop machine gutted to make a large cooler for food storage. This was where we ate and gathered to sing songs, but most importantly, it was home base when we played "Run-Sheep-Run," my favorite camping game.

The family tent section lay north of the meeting area; it always amazed me, the different tents people would bring. Some families shared big army tents, others two-person pup tents. My family had recently purchased an eight-person tent from Sears with screened windows and flaps to cover them at night.

The first duty of camping as a large group is to expedite the erecting of everyone's tent. My father and I tried to assemble our tent first by reading the directions, but we eventually gave up and just started putting pieces together. After a couple of mistakes, we finally finished by pounding the tent stakes in, then we headed off to see if anyone else needed help.

The teenage girls and young women's area lay east of the meeting area, its boundaries separated by clotheslines and sheets, and labeled, "Private Restricted Area, Stay Out!" Inevitably, it was the last area to go to sleep, and always required a few stern words from a mother or two, to remind them to be quiet.

The placement of the teenage boys and young men's site lay to the west of the meeting area—no tents, just sleeping bags laid out on the ground. I considered it a rite of passage to sleep in this area, and I hoped my father would let me sleep at least one night with the older boys this weekend.

To the south of the meeting area lay the volleyball court and the horseshoe pits; this was hallowed ground where great battles of skill were waged all day long and often into the night. I couldn't wait to show I was a year older and stronger and ready to be a valued teammate, or worthy opponent. Some might have described me as a skinny or wiry kid, but competitive blood pumped through my veins.

My full extended family arrived for the weekend: cousins, aunts and uncles, and half the people from our church. The women were all gabbing about women things: cooking, knitting, and babies. Most of the men were playing horseshoes. My older cousins had gone off to the swimming hole, but my cousin Tim and I had to stay behind because we happened to be in trouble again.

Our younger cousin Lyle constantly followed us like a lost puppy. Being a year and a half older and tired of babysitting him, we decided to teach him a lesson by playing a prank on him.

In the area where the men played horseshoes, there was a bees' nest hidden underground. The bees didn't seem to mind all the commotion as long as you didn't get too close to their nest. When Tim and I asked Lyle if he wanted to go watch the men play, Lyle's face lit up and his tail started wagging. Tim and I sat down next to the bees' nest, and we motioned to Lyle to sit between us, which he did, right on top of the entrance of the nest. It didn't take long before Lyle got stung several times on the butt, for which Tim and I received as many swats on our behinds. We apologized, but we still had to stand facing a tree for what seemed like forever.

While standing and not speaking, I overheard my Aunt Sarah talking to my mother. Aunt Sarah's voice was quivering like someone trying to sing falsetto, so I turned to look. Trembling and crying, Aunt Sarah told my mom my cousin Dennis had flunked senior English because he failed to turn in his assignment on the novel *A Tale of Two Cities*, and now he would not graduate from high school with the rest of his class.

"He must take summer school to receive his diploma," Aunt Sarah said. "But Dennis is refusing to attend."

To occupy my time as I stood facing the tree, I practiced counting by tens. I made it to twenty-five thousand before my mother excused us. Tim and I played catch for a while then decided to go swimming. We thought about going fishing, but the best times to fish are early mornings and right before dusk, not in the middle of the day. What we were both looking forward to the most was the weekend's first night of Run-Sheep-Run.

When dusk set in, the evening activities began. Cookies, hot chocolate, and coffee adorned several picnic tables, and large slabs of wood fueled the campfire. Once everyone settled in, the evening sing-along commenced. The band consisted of a harmonica, a six-string guitar, and a Jew's harp. The honor of song leading belonged to my father. In high school, he sang in a local quartet, and for many years, led the worship service at church. The songs we sang around the campfire encompassed a variety of folk and Sunday school songs. I loved singing, whether it was at church, at home, or around the campfire. Dad always sang around the house and at work, and I was a chip off the old block. I knew every song by heart, and I belted them out like a star on the Grand Ole Opry.

With the sing-along over, we could finally get to the best thing about going camping, playing Run-Sheep-Run. By this time, the fire had burned down to a red-hot cone of coals, and while you could see the campfire from a hundred feet away, its illumination encompassed a much smaller circle. It was time to choose teams.

The customary selection of captains preceded the process; tonight my father and Dennis would establish the teams. The players quickly formed small groups of four to six players, and then the captains selected groups to make up their teams. Dad then explained to the newcomers the rules, and the object of the game.

"One captain will take his sheep (team) out and hide them in the woods," he said, "While the other captain and his sheep remain here at the campfire, which is home base. Once the hiding team's captain conceals his sheep, the captain returns to home base, and the game commences."

"Using his arms, the hiding team's captain will point in two different directions. One arm will point to where his team is hiding, while the other arm will be a false position."

"The object for the hiding team is to make it back to home base undetected. The object of the other team, the hunting team, is to find the hiding sheep, and then beat them back to home base in a foot race."

"The team who gets all their members back to home base first is the winner."

"Once the team who is hunting begins their search, the captain of the hiding team will begin calling out signals for his team. "Pancakes" could mean retreat slowly, while "Applesauce" could mean lay low. "Green" could mean go right, and "Red" could mean advance quickly."

"In the darkness, a well-hidden team can escape the detection of the other team if they remain calm and silent; hence, stealth is the key to winning."

"If the hiding team's captain thinks his team is closer to home base than the hunting team, he'll call out, "Run, sheep, run."

"If someone on the hunting team spots the hiding team, they call out, "Run, sheep, run," and either way the race is on."

"If the hiding team wins, they depart to go hide again. If the hunting team wins, they rally, then go hide."

Tim and I, along with Austin, were on Dennis's team. Dennis and Austin had done some reconnaissance earlier in the day; together they located a good place to hide, and devised a plan of how to navigate back to the campfire without detection. Dennis led us away from the campfire in one direction, but once we disappeared out of the visual range of the other team, we circled around to the opposite side. We hid in a field of tall ferns; we had room to move either right, left, or backward, and a stand of thick under-brush protected us from a direct line of pursuit.

Dennis's plan included options. If they chose the false position, we'd retrace our steps the way we had come. If they chose our true location, we'd wait and see which direction they came around the thick underbrush and then move in the opposite direction. Before he left, he gave us our signals, "Blueberries" meant stay put, "Hard-boiled eggs" meant proceed cautiously, "Yellow" meant move forward, "Purple" meant retreat, "Coca-Cola" meant go right, and "Root beer" meant go left, and "Run, sheep, run" meant run as fast you can to home base. We all believed Dennis's signals would work if things proceeded as planned, but if the plan fell apart, we knew Dennis would be shouting directions based upon where he thought we were, not our actual location. Without question, from that point forward, our chances of success would rely on our plan, not Dennis's signals.

My father knew the way Dennis had left was a decoy, so he chose our true location and his team began tromping toward us. We could hear them from seventy-five yards away. We waited, then Dennis called out his first signal, "Blueberries, blueberries, blueberries," which meant to stay put. Next, he shouted, "The Flintstones," which didn't mean anything. Finally, he yelled, "Coca-Cola" and "Hard-boiled eggs," and we began circling our way around to the right.

Dennis kept calling, "Coca-Cola," and we kept retracing our steps just as Dennis had planned, until Dad's team turned around and headed in the other direction, running as fast as they could. Dennis began calling out "Purple, purple, purple." We could hear them approaching, so we fell flat on our stomachs and began crawling on our hands and knees away from their advance. Luckily, someone on Dad's team thought they heard something, and they rushed off away from us. Dennis once again started calling out, "Coca-Cola," and we quickly began to move toward home base. Suddenly, Dennis called out, "Run, sheep, run." Our team took off sprinting as fast as we could. Tim was running right beside me when I must have hit a tree root with my foot, and before I could catch myself, I began doing somersaults head over heels. Tim stopped and helped me up, and then we both continued running. Even with my fall, we still managed to be the first two to arrive for our team. The rest of our team began trickling in, not far behind us, but as they continued to stream in, members from my father's team began arriving. Finally, the last members of our team reached home base and we all cheered.

It was such a good win; we decided to let the losing team hide instead of us. All total, we won three times the first night, and my father's team won only once. We decided to call it quits sometime shortly after midnight. At that point, everyone began making their way back to their tents and sleeping areas. Dad and I stayed a few minutes longer to extinguish the fire before heading to our tent.

My sisters were fast asleep by the time we arrived; I crawled into my sleeping bag and said good night to my parents. After my dad settled in, I heard Mom tell him, "Dennis isn't going to graduate." I could hear Dad recoil at this news; he unzipped his side of their sleeping bag, uncovered himself, and laid there with his hands clasped together behind his head while Mom and he continued to talk. Dennis was Dad's favorite nephew, and Dad often told stories of the tricks he use to play on a much younger

Dennis. My father was the only child to graduate from high school of the six children in his family, and now the oldest family member of the next generation had failed to do so. As I laid there with my hands clasped behind my head, I promised myself I would never let my father down. I'd graduate from high school.

I'm not sure about the other things Mom and Dad talked about because my eyelids refused to stay open, but I did hear something about the possibility of Dad giving Dennis a job.

My father and my Grandpa owned a gravel-and-concrete business, and they called its location the "Plant." In my mind, it constituted the greatest place on earth, a place where big boys played with real life-sized Tonka Trucks and construction equipment. My favorite thing to do was ride along with my father when he delivered rock or cement to someone's house. I may have been only nine, but those days have always remained some of the best days of my life. My father's job looked like play to me, but he worked long, hard hours, and after he got home from work, there never seemed to be enough time to play or visit before I had to go to bed. The trips with my father were his way of replacing that lost time; they were extra special, better than catching a fish, which was my second-favorite thing to do.

On Sunday night, the last night of the holiday weekend, Tim and I asked our parents if we could sleep among the older boys, and they said yes. When the last game of Run-Sheep-Run was finished, we both raced to where we had stashed our sleeping bags and joined the older boys on the walk back to their designated sleeping area. When we arrived, Austin threw a few twigs into the campfire pit, and as they began to smolder, Dennis told us to lay out our bags and then hurry back. When Tim and I returned, everyone stopped talking.

Rick said, "Those who sleep here have a special bond, and new members must prove themselves worthy."

Austin looked into our eyes and said, "To prove your worth, you must complete a task we give you successfully."

"You must creep over to where the watermelons are chilling for tomorrow's lunch," Dennis said, "And steal a nice, large, ripe one without being caught." They then gave us a small flashlight and sent us on our way.

In our magical camping kingdom, there's a spring from which ice-cold, sweet-tasting water bubbles up from the ground. This is where our drinking water came from; it's also where the watermelons chilled. One of our Memorial Day traditions included a watermelon feast after lunch before everyone started packing up to go home. Every family brought a watermelon or two and placed it in the spring, in advance of the feast.

As quietly as possible, Tim and I made our way through the pitch-black night with only the tiny flashlight to help us. When we reached the spring, Tim reached in and fished out a large, firm melon; we both grasped an end, and with the flashlight clinched between my teeth, we started back. We hadn't taken more than four or five steps when two blinding beams of light split the darkness, and a voice yelled, "What are you doing!"

I dropped my end of the watermelon and the flashlight, and Tim and I lit out on a dead sprint, running as fast as our little legs could run. We stumbled through the underbrush, fearing the worst, and hoping for a miracle. Out of breath, we reached the older boys' campfire and began explaining what had happened, until the other boys broke out into a ruckus of laughter. Dennis and Austin described the look on our faces when they turned on their flashlights, and everyone began laughing again. Rick then brought out the watermelon we had dropped and sliced it into individual pieces; as the two newest members of the Big Boys Club, Rick presented Tim and me the first two slices, as Dennis and Austin provided another instant replay of the whole incident one more time.

Tim and I were now official members of the Big Boys Club.

The next day, as the whole camp gathered for the Watermelon Feast, Dennis and Austin were still laughing.

As I spit watermelon seeds and tossed watermelon rinds, I started to feel lonely again, knowing the long holiday weekend was over, but then, to my surprise, as everyone began packing up to go home, I saw Dennis put his stuff with my families. I could hardly believe it, Dennis was coming to live with us and work for Dad and Grandpa. Like a kid with ants in his pants, I couldn't stand still; I had a smile on my face as wide as the Grand Canyon; I was going to have a big brother.

– 1 –

The First Summer

MOM AND DAD had started an addition to our small house that spring. The walls had siding on them and the roof was finished, but there was no heat or electricity as of yet; it became Dennis's house. There was no opening between our house and Dennis's house at the time, so each evening, Dennis had to go outside and make his way through the darkness to the new addition. The first night as he passed by my sister's bedroom he pressed his face to the window and they screamed, and then he did the same to mine. It became an evening tradition we all looked forward to and missed, if he forgot, or he came home from work too late and we were already sleeping.

Dennis had some special talents, a few rituals, and one great love. One of the special talents he performed repeatedly for us that summer was drinking a 16 oz. bottle of

Coke in one gulp without stopping to breathe. He'd take a few deep breaths, lift the glass bottle to a vertical position, tip his head back, and let it flow. One of his other rituals was to plop two Alka-Seltzers into a glass of water, and drink the bicarbonate after he finished dinner. In both cases, the result was a long, loud belch.

Another of Dennis's many talents was cooking. One morning he introduced my sisters and me to chocolate chip, peanut butter, coconut pancakes, which quickly became a household favorite. Looking back it might have been his weird food concoctions that caused him to use so much bicarbonate.

Dennis's greatest talent, if it is a talent, and one of the great joys of his young life, was his ability to hitchhike. Dennis could get anywhere by sticking out his thumb. He could get a ride from nearly any stranger driving by. I don't know if it was his friendly smile, or how he held his thumb out, but I'm sure no one was as good at it as he was.

Dennis's great love was baseball, he loved playing it, he loved watching it, he loved everything about the game. We spent hours in the field behind our house tossing the ball and playing catch. Sometimes Dad would join us and we'd play some kind of modified game. Dennis's love for the game came from sitting on our great grandfather's lap and watching the "Saturday baseball game of the week" and hearing him tell his baseball stories. Great Grandpa in his twenties had been a major league ball player for the St. Louis Browns, a team long-forgotten by most people but not by Dennis or Great Grandpa.

During WWI, a few major league ball players were drafted, and others volunteered for service, leaving room for a few good minor league players to move up to the majors. Grandpa was a catcher and supposedly a very good one. He had played for the University of Michigan while earning a degree in engineering. Upon graduation, his parents' expectation was that he would get an engineering job, but Great Grandpa wanted to continue playing baseball, and worse, he wanted to marry a young girl he'd met at college. Great Grandpa's parents didn't approve of her or baseball, and were so angry with him when he signed a baseball contract and married the girl, they disowned him. The story I heard is he and Great Grandma left and supposedly never talked to Great Grandpa's parents again.

Great Grandpa was an up-and-coming player as far as the Browns were concerned, but too many collisions at home plate caused him to lose his hearing in one ear, which kept him out of military service during the war, but allowed him to fulfill his dreams of playing major league baseball. When the war ended, the Browns demoted Great Grandpa back to the minors. Before the start of the next season, he was traded to the Yankees, but they cut him because of his hearing loss, and he never played major league ball again. The St. Louis Browns would later move to Baltimore, Maryland, and become the Orioles. Great Grandpa and Grandma moved to California. While Great Grandpa never played a major league game for the Yankees, he and Dennis would become life-long fans of the Bronx Bombers.

From the first day, Dennis played little league, people said he was special. It could be Grandpa endowed him with his spirit of baseball, or with his genes, but for whatever reason, Dennis was a natural. Big for his age, he was an all-star throughout little league and Babe Ruth. Dad took me to watch him play one of his high school games. He hit a double and a home run. His high school coach said he could have played college ball or signed a semi-pro contract after high school, but life doesn't always turn out like you want, or how you've planned.

A few days after Dennis moved in with us, school got out for the summer. It seemed like forever since last summer, and I couldn't wait to be free again to play. Mom picked up my sisters and me from school on the last day, and took us shopping for summer clothes. As we shopped, she explained she had signed us up for the school's summer reading program, and she expected us to read several books during our summer vacation.

The school had an old bus they had converted into a library on wheels; they called it "The Bookmobile." The program provided books to students who didn't live in town, or didn't have access to the community public library during the summer. The Bookmobile stopped at our house every two weeks during that summer. The first book I checked out was *Where the Red Fern Grows.* It was a little hard for me to read, but Mom helped me with the words I couldn't pronounce. Once I started reading it, I didn't want to stop. The story captured my interest and my heart. One night, Mom and Dad came into my room after I'd gone to bed because they heard me crying. They asked me what was wrong, and I told them I'd been thinking about the book, and I didn't want the dogs Old Dan and Little Ann to die. Dad explained to me it was just a book and not real, but I could see tears in Mom's eyes as well.

Our family had a cocker spaniel named Goldie. She loved to lick your hands and face, and for the next few days, I spent extra time playing with her and petting her. She wasn't a hunting dog like Old Dan or Little Ann, but she was our dog. Two weeks later, when the Bookmobile returned, I turned the book back in, and checked out *Treasure Island.*

Working for Dad and Grandpa required the use of every muscle group in your body. Dennis said, "It felt like you'd fought a fifteen-round heavyweight fight by the end of the day." Dad knew it was hard work, so he tried to mix in some levity with the drudgery.

Dennis's first job took him almost two weeks to complete. Several months earlier, the motor that turned the barrel on one of Dad's cement trucks had failed, with a full load of cement inside, the cement quickly hardened into concrete, which now required a chisel and hammer for removal. Dennis had to crawl through a small opening to get inside the barrel, which he barely fit through, and once inside, he had to break up the concrete into small pieces and roll the chunks down the chute. The other men who worked for Dad took a liking to Dennis and always made sure to pound on the outside of the barrel as they passed by, which made it reverberate like a bass drum on the inside. One time, Grandpa hadn't heard any pounding for a while, so he peeked inside to see what was going on, and found Dennis sound asleep. He decided to wake him up by shoving a water hose up inside the barrel and turning it on full blast. Dennis came climbing out of the barrel, ready to fight the perpetrator of this joke, only to find Grandpa laughing hysterically at him.

After dinner was finished, my sisters and I always asked Dennis to play. He often volunteered to take my two oldest sisters and me down to the river to swim. During the winter, Dad would use his big shovel, which looked like a crane, to take gravel out the river; this made big holes that filed up with water. They were perfect for swimming in during the summer. Neighbors from the surrounding area would often come down to the river during the evenings to swim and cool off on the hot summer nights. It was also the hot spot for teenage girls to sunbathe, which is probably why Dennis was so willing to volunteer to take his young cousins swimming.

– 2 –

DAD PAID HIS employees every two weeks. Dennis received his first paycheck at four o'clock on Friday, and by five o'clock, he had hitchhiked back to his home in Longview. He caught a ride to the freeway with the first car headed to town, and within minutes, flagged down another ride that took him the remaining twenty-some miles. He shoveled some food into his mouth, took a bath, and by six o'clock, was uptown in a friend's car, cruising main street, all due to his amazing hitchhiking thumb. On Sunday after church, Dennis would ride home with us, but after work every other Friday, he'd hitchhike back home to Longview.

After chipping all the concrete out of the cement barrel, Dennis's next job was more pleasant. Dad taught him how to run the rock crusher. He would use the scoop-mobile to load up the big hopper with river-run rock, and then start the huge, electric motors that ran the crusher. The sound the rock crusher made reverberated across the plant. It sounded like a fist hitting a punching bag repeatedly, as the crushed rock became smaller and smaller fragments. The river-run rock from the hopper ran through the crusher and then fell on to a belt, which then dumped it into a large screen that separated the sand and rock by size. The only responsibility the operator had was to make sure the rock crusher didn't clog, and if it did, to hit the kill switch that turned off the electric motors and then unclog it. My job was to pluck sticks. Grandpa welded a seat onto the crusher frame next to the moving belt so I could snare the pieces of wood as they passed by. Besides plucking sticks, I constantly scanned the moving belt for agates and other pretty rocks. Grandpa gave me a nickel for the real pretty ones. Most of the other operators just sat under the umbrella with their eyes half closed. But Dennis ran the rock crusher with the radio on, the volume turned up as loud as it would go, on a station that played the Top Hits of the '60s. He always sang along with the Beach Boys songs; soon, so did I.

One afternoon, when I showed up at the plant to deliver a message to my father from my mother, I found Dennis alone, cleaning tools and organizing supplies. A few minutes later, another cousin of ours, Rick, stopped by the plant.

Rick had a mischievous side. He once convinced me to sell him a silver dollar for two fifty-cent pieces. My parents didn't make Rick give it back, even though the silver dollar was worth much more than a dollar. They had instructed me not to show it to other people or to take it to the store or sell it; the loss taught me two things: one, to listen to my parents, and two, sometimes, one item can be more valuable than two.

On this day, Rick wanted Dennis to help him start an old pickup that sat around the plant so they could race. The white 1946 Ford had bald tires, the seat springs were sticking through the seat, and the windshield looked like a spiderweb. However, it ran, if you had a fully charged battery and you dumped a little gas in the carburetor before you tried to start it. It was lightweight with a six-cylinder motor and a challenge for Rick's 1952 V-8 Pontiac. They told me if I swore not to tell my father, I could ride with Dennis. I promised, and I never said a word. This would not be the only secret ever kept between Dennis and me. Another secret I kept for years would come out later.

I received a new fishing pole and reel for my birthday that summer. The reel had a button you held down when you started your cast, and then you released it as you cast. I tied a one-ounce sinker on to the end of the line, and was practicing casting in our front yard. After several minutes of practicing, Dennis asked if he could try it, but on his first try, he took his finger off the button too soon and instead of the sinker going forward, the sinker went backward, right through the large plate glass window in the front of our house. I got into so much trouble, but I never told my parents it was Dennis.

At first, I felt disappointed Dennis didn't 'fess up and take responsibility, but after I didn't tattletale on him, we seemed to become much closer. He really became my big brother.

Each day that summer, I delivered lunch to my father and Dennis. We only lived about a quarter mile from the plant, so Mom would make their lunches about 11:00 a.m. and I'd walk or ride my bike over to the plant. Dad usually let the employees have some extra time to have fun after lunch, if all the morning deliveries were completed. We'd play basketball at a hoop they had put up in the shop, or sometimes we'd go swimming. However, having rock skipping contests was my favorite. We all tried, but no one could beat my father. I'd been around other fathers who let their kids win, but my father never did. If I lost, I was never sad, just more determined to win the next time. I think it instilled in me a competitive spirit, a spirit I've always kept.

At one of these lunches, Dennis introduced "The Greatest Game" to everyone. He explained the game, and then we began. The topic was "America's Greatest Landmark," we drew straws, and Grandpa drew the short straw.

"America's greatest landmark is Mount Rushmore," Grandpa said. "Gutzon Borglum carved the faces of George Washington, Thomas Jefferson, Teddy Roosevelt, and Abraham Lincoln into a lime stone mountain in South Dakota. These presidents epitomize the first 150 years of American history. It's one of most visited places in America, so it has to be America's greatest landmark!"

Chuck spoke next, "There's no doubt in my mind the answer is the Empire State Building, America's first great skyscraper. Its construction began in 1930, and took only a little over a year. It set the standard for American architecture and engineering, and the future look of New York City's skyline."

"My choice is Hoover Dam," Dad said. "Built during the Great Depression it took 3,250,000 yards of concrete to build it. The greatest continuous pour of cement ever attempted at the time."

I said, "How did I know you would choose something that had to do with concrete?"

Dennis shared next. "The greatest American landmark is the Panama Canal."

"That's not in America," Grandpa said.

"I didn't say it had to be in the United States."

Grandpa responded, "We see how you play!"

"The Panama Canal's construction was started by a French company, but an American company completed the job, and it is located in Central America. The completion of the Panama Canal changed the world. Ships no longer had to go around the southern tip of South America."

I proposed my selection next, "My Choice is the Seattle Space Needle; I saw it at the 1962 World's Fair." I didn't know anymore, so I left it at that.

Clarence submitted his choice last. He said, "The White House is definitely the best answer. Over the last fifty years, I bet more people have visited it than any other American landmark."

Dennis said, "It's now time to vote. Raise your hand if you think Mount Rushmore is the greatest American landmark. Now those for the Empire State Building. Raise your hand for Hoover Dam. The Panama Canal, no one! Raise your hand if you think its the Space Needle. Lastly, raise your hand if you're voting for The White House. With three votes, the winner is Chuck and the Empire State building."

It was the first time I'd played The Greatest Game, but I would remember it years later when we'd play it again.

On the Fourth of July, we got up early and our family, including Dennis, drove to Longview for the annual church picnic. Upon arrival, I spotted Tim, and we ran to the horseshoe pits to be first. We'd practice from half the distance, and then from three-quarters distance so we would be ready when we were strong enough to pitch the shoes the full distance.

This Fourth of July seemed different from others, people seem to be wearing long faces and speaking in hushed voices. The somber mood dampened the festivities like a cloud-filled sky threatening to rain, but there were no clouds, the sky was as blue as blue can be. There was a great deal of talk about the war. I didn't know much about it, but I had seen reports about it on the evening news. As a nine-year-old, my idea of war consisted of playing cowboys and Indians: you shot the bad people with your finger until everyone fell down, and then everybody got up and you did it all over again. I knew my father had been in the Korean War, because I'd heard him tell a few stories about it now and then, but his stories were always funny, never danger-ous, or sad.

Most people were talking about how the government had started drafting eighteen and nineteen-year-olds. Some of the parents from church were talking about send-ing their sons to college so they wouldn't have to fight.

Dennis tried to liven up the somberness of the day by bringing out the firecrackers, the Whistling Pete's, and the Sparkling Cones he'd bought. Soon, we were all laughing until one of the cones tipped over and started the grass on fire. The grass was dry, and the fire spread very quickly. Several of us tried to stomp the fire out with our shoes while others used rakes and shovels. The fire continued to spread rapidly until someone hooked up a garden hose and put out the fire. With the fire finally extinguished, every-one stopped and took a deep breath. Then Dennis started laughing; it seemed the holiday spirit had returned, but not everyone thought it was funny. A high level of tension remained for the next few hours as people realized just how close the fire had come to catching the church on fire. There were no more fireworks on this Fourth of July.

The minister took the opportunity to use an analogy of the fire started by the fireworks in his afternoon message. The fire represented hell and the Fourth of July represented Freedom, the type of freedom only found through the salvation provided by God's Son, Jesus Christ. I may not have known what an analogy was at the time, but I understood hell was a bad place, and I didn't want to go there.

We had a quiet evening trip home; my sisters had fallen asleep as soon as the car began moving. I sat in the back seat with them, my parents and Dennis were in the front seat. My parents didn't speak much on the way home, which was odd. I wasn't sure if it was just from the long day, or because of dissatisfaction with Dennis's carelessness with the fireworks. No one ever openly spoke about it, but I always got the feeling that if the church had actually caught on fire, the blame would have fallen on Dennis.

Dad's business was a quarter mile from our house in one direction, and less than a quarter mile away in the opposite direction was Clover Valley Sunday School. The church building, a former schoolhouse, had an auditorium, classrooms, and a separate gym. They held Sunday school services there every Sunday morning, starting at 10:00 a.m., they would ring the old school bell at nine, and again at nine-thirty to remind any of community members who might have slept in. We weren't regular members because we attended church in Longview, but my father sometimes played basketball with other adults in the gym—that was always open for community members to use.

The church offered vacation Bible school every summer, and my sisters and I always attended. There was a walking path along the road, running between our house and the church. You could stand at the end of our driveway and visually see the church from there. My mother would walk us each morning to the church and meet us at our driveway when Bible school was over. As soon as we left the church, we could see her, and she would wave to us. I remember the number one rule was to hold my sister's hand, and the second rule was not to cross the road until Mom walked us across. I didn't mind the rules; I knew they were for my sister because I crossed the road by myself to take my father his lunch each day.

The thoughts of the minister's message on the Fourth of July kept coming back to me each day during vacation Bible school as I heard the stories from the Bible. One story struck a chord in my heart. Nicodemus, a Jewish leader, came to Jesus one night to ask him questions.

He said, "I know God has sent you to teach us, your miracles are proof enough of this."

Jesus replied, "I tell you this; unless you are born again, you can never enter into the Kingdom of God."

"Do you mean I must enter my mother's womb and be born again?" Nicodemus asked.

"You must be born of water and the Spirit," Jesus said, "Men can only reproduce, but the Holy Spirit gives new life from heaven."

"What do you mean?" Nicodemus said.

"There is no eternal doom awaiting those who trust God to save them," Jesus said, "But those who don't trust God, have already been tried and condemned for not believing in the only Son of God."

I hated spankings; I learned at an early age the threat of pain was a great deterrent to misbehavior. It was simple logic to me, each of us have a choice of where we will spend eternity, hell or heaven. Hell's a terrible place full of misery and pain. Heaven's a place of love and joy.

As a child, I thought like a child, but as I matured as a person and as a Christian, I learned God's love is not about pain versus joy, but about love. The true question is, do we wish to experience God's love here on earth and throughout eternity? Or never know God's love for us here on earth and be totally separated from his love and presence for eternity when we die?

So on Thursday, when the pastor asked for those who wanted to give their life to Jesus to come forward, I had no doubts, I wanted to accept Jesus into my heart, so I went forward. Besides me, eight others came forward on that day, including my sister. There was happiness, but not the kind you feel when you get the Christmas present you were hoping for. I felt different, like the biggest decision of my life had been taken care of, and I had no more fear of the future. I knew Jesus was in my heart to stay forever and if I died, I'd go to heaven and not hell.

My sister had also decided to accept Jesus, and I knew our parents would be excited, because they were Christians and wanted us to be. They had been teaching us about God's love since we were little. We could hardly wait to tell them. As soon as we crossed the road together, Beth blurted out the news. Mom told us Dad would be very glad about this, and to celebrate, she was going to make our favorite dessert.

Dad and Dennis got home from work about six-thirty. Mom had the food already on the table, so they washed up and sat down as quickly as possible. After Dad said grace, Mom said, "Before we begin, Nathan and Beth have some good news to share."

I looked at Beth and she motioned for me to go first, so I said, "At vacation Bible school today, they asked those who wanted to accept Jesus as their Savior to come forward, so I did, and I asked Jesus into my heart."

Beth chimed in, "I did too!"

Our father smiled, and then he got up and gave us both big hugs and kisses. He told us he was proud of us, and after dinner, we'd get the family Bible out, and enter today's date and write a little statement that we had accepted Jesus today. We could both then sign our names next to it.

After dinner, Dad opened the family Bible, and turned it to the pages where our names were entered on the day we were born. He wrote below each of our names the sentence, "Let it be known, on this date, they have been born again, this time of the Spirit," after which, we printed our names. Dad then said a prayer, and Mom brought out the dessert, blackberry pie and ice cream.

As we were eating, I asked Dennis if he was a Christian. There was a moment of silence, as if I had asked an inappropriate question. Then finally, in an uneasy voice, as if he had never been asked the question before, or at least not for a long time, he answered, "Yes."

He said, "A long time ago, when your father was my Sunday school teacher."

I didn't ask any more questions, but I looked at my father and he was smiling.

Then I did ask, "Can we play baseball now?"

The next few weeks were full of fun. It was mid-summer, the days were warm and long, and Mom took my sisters and me to the swimming hole every afternoon, except on the days I worked at the plant. On those days, after dinner, the whole family, including Dennis, would usually go swimming. I don't know what it is about swimming, but I can never get enough of it. My parents used to call me a water dog.

On one of these evenings, I took a challenge that wasn't meant for me, but I accepted without others realizing it. My uncle was challenging a local teenager to swim the length of the swimming hole and back without stopping. I thought he was talking to me, and I was sure I could make it, so I dove off the dock and began swimming.

The length of the swimming hole was at least a hundred yards long and fifteen to twenty feet deep in the center. I had never swum half of that distance before at one time, but I wasn't going to let anyone call me a baby or a chicken, so off I paddled. At first, I swam freestyle, and when I got tired, I turned on my side, and then on to my back. I reached the other end and began the return leg; about then, a few people standing on the dock realized what I was doing.

I could hear people shouting, I thought I heard my mom screaming at my dad, but I didn't know why. I was concentrating on swimming, and I was tired. Suddenly, I heard someone swimming toward me as fast as they could, I was swimming on my back, and when I turned my head, Dennis was there, asking me if I needed help. I told him I could make it; I only had about twenty more yards to go. He said, "I know you can, do you mind if I swim alongside of you?"

I told him, "I'd like that." After what seemed like an hour, I finally reached the dock again. Dennis helped me up on to the dock because I had so little strength left.

He said, "That was quite a feat, I'm not sure I could do it." I knew he could, but it made me feel like a million bucks.

I was so tired, I just laid there on the dock face up with the water lapping against my body, and then I began to shiver. It was eighty-five degrees out, but I couldn't stop shaking. My father who had helped pull me out of the water and hadn't left my side, now picked me up and carried me to the shore, where my mom wrapped me in a blanket. It took time, but I began to warm up. It would be a couple of more summers before I would attempt the challenge again. Nevertheless, everyone knew I could do it!

— 3 —

A COUPLE OF weeks before my birthday, Dad and I made our once-a-month trip into town on Saturday morning to get haircuts. Getting a haircut was a community event in our town. You arrived at the barber shop, took your seat, and waited your turn. A ten-minute trim required an hour's wait, but there was always the latest community news and the high school sports to talk about. I usually just sat and listened and looked through the magazines and newspapers as I waited, but this Saturday morning, something caught my eye—a photograph of a dog. His name was Champ and his breed elkhound; he had a face that looked like a small bear's face, a curled tail, and his eyes were full of life. There was also a small story about how Champ could be adopted. I showed the picture and story to my father who looked at it but didn't say much, other than Champ looked like a nice dog. I never made a big deal about it, and when our haircuts were finished, we headed back home after our traditional stop for ice cream.

During the summer, Mom and Dad continued to work on completing the addition to the house. They installed the windows and painted the siding, but the most important thing, the wiring for electricity, was completed. Dennis now had lights and an electrical outlet. The next Sunday, when we came home, Dennis brought with him his record player, and his collection of 45s. Soon my sisters and I were singing along to the Beach Boys, the Beatles, and the best music of the early sixties. I learned every word to "She Was Just Seventeen," "I Want to Hold Your Hand," and "Surfing USA," I can still remember the words to those songs today, and I still sing along when I hear them on the radio.

It was a summer full of lessons for Dennis; he learned how to run the rock crusher, how to batch out cement, and drive a dump truck. He left for work at 5:30 a.m. and returned home usually for dinner by 6:30 p.m., but every other Friday, as soon as work was over, he'd make a beeline for the highway, put out his thumb, and hitchhike his way back home for the weekend. This is not to say there weren't a few bumps in the road, like the time he decided to learn how to drive a dump truck without permission. He wound up side swiping another truck parked in the lot. Dad made Dennis pound out the dents in the fenders, then putty and sand them smooth, all on his own time and without pay. When he had properly completed the job, Dad taught him how to drive a dump truck, and when Dad was satisfied

Dennis could drive it safely, he put him to work as an in-lot driver and raised his pay.

There was also the time Grandpa fired him. Grandpa, who didn't work every day, showed up without notice, and caught Dennis racing Rick in the old '46 Ford pickup. Grandpa fired Dennis and forbade Rick to be on the property during business hours. As Dennis described what happened to Dad, he said Grandpa's face was red and turning purple, the wrinkles in his forehead were bulging, and he had to stop for breaths while shouting at them at the top of his lungs.

Grandpa wasn't upset with Dennis because he should have been working instead of goofing around with Rick. He was upset because he feared for their safety.

Grandpa said, "I could never forgive myself if there was an accident, and one or both of you were injured, or worse, killed."

Dad made Dennis walk the half-mile between our house and Grandpa's to apologize and ask for his job back. I heard Dennis tell Dad later it was the hardest thing he'd ever done. After Dennis apologized, and before he got back to our house, Grandpa called Dad. They were both laughing about the whole situation. I heard my Father say, "I'm sure he's learned his lesson." I also know by the end of the week the old '46 Ford was gone and no one ever questioned where it went.

I learned a lesson as well: I could have easily have been riding along with Dennis on that day, as I had before, and then I would have been in trouble too. Then we both would have had to face not only the wrath of Grandpa but also my father's, and I don't think there would have been any laughing. I never considered what we were doing as being dangerous, but in hindsight, two vehicles with bald tires chasing each other on a dirt road with huge bumps around tight turns, lined by old growth trees while not wearing seatbelts was not too bright.

One late afternoon, not long before quitting time, one of the employees while loading sand from the sand pit into Dennis's dump truck struck something unusual, it was a large mound of rocks that had been laid in a circular pattern. To everyone there, this was clearly not a natural occurrence, but something man-made. Not wanting to disturb it any further, they stopped working in the area for the day. By the time Dad returned, everyone had gone home. However, when Dad arrived at our house, Dennis met him at the door to tell him all about the discovery. Dad was all excited and phoned Grandpa, and then we all jumped into the car and raced to the sand pit where Grandpa met us.

With hand shovels Dad, Grandpa, and Dennis began to unearth the structure of rocks. Whatever its purpose, it was about five feet wide and three feet deep. Before much more could be determined, it became too dark to continue.

Grandpa went home to pick up Grandma, and then they followed us back to our house. Everyone was guessing about what it could be. Grandpa thought it could be an unmarked grave of one of the original settlers of the area. Dennis agreed it could be a grave, but he thought it was more likely to be an Indian grave, maybe even a chief.

He said, "I've read about how Pacific Northwest Indian tribes often buried their dead by covering them with rocks so animals couldn't dig up their bodies."

Dad disagreed and had his own theory. He told us the story an old man who lived nearby had told him.

Dad said, "One day, the old man and him were visiting, and the old man said, see those crows, they just flew over a large pot of gold."

Dad asked him what he meant, and the old man revealed the following details, "During the Great Depression, President Franklin Roosevelt created public works projects to put people to work. One of those projects was the building of a hydroelectric dam a few miles upriver. The project employed hundreds of men, most of them single and from other parts of the region. The woman, who owned Grandpa's land at the time, built a large house with lots of bedrooms." Today, it's my grandparents' house. He said, "She then set up a roadhouse that sold liquor, had gambling tables, and ladies of the evening. She and her associates had a thriving business until the dam was finished. But, after the workers left, the profits dropped off, so she turned her attention to a new scheme.

"She had a rich uncle who lived back east who was sick, and she convinced him clean, fresh air and sunshine would cure his ills, and she invited him to come live with her. She knew he distrusted banks, having lost a large portion of his wealth to their failure after the stock market crash of 1929. He took her up on the offer, and came west along with $80,000 in five, ten, and twenty dollar gold pieces.

"Soon after arriving, he discovered she had lied to him, and described her home as a prison. She didn't allow him to go anywhere except for short walks along the river.

"One day, the man met me when I was fishing, and he poured his soul out to me, fearing her plans included murder and the theft of his gold. Together, we hatched a plan to bury the gold to keep it safe. We dug a hole, lined it with rocks, and placed a crock with the gold coins inside into the hole, and then we covered the crock with rocks, and then dirt."

The old man said, "His fellow neighbor one day just disappeared, never to be seen again."

When he asked about him, she claimed he had returned to the East.

But the old man said, "If that were true, he would have taken his money with him, and he had checked and the ground where they had buried it had not been disturbed."

He said, "She murdered him, but she never found the money."

I asked my father why the neighbor didn't take the money, since he knew where it was.

Dad said, "He was an old man, and the gold didn't mean much to him."

I said, "If that's true, why didn't he tell you where the gold was at?"

He said "He was afraid I'd dig it up and spend it on a fast car. The old man had lost his only son to an automobile accident, so he refused to tell me where it was, but he insisted it was still there."

Having heard the story, I couldn't sleep that night. I couldn't wait to find out if we had our own *Treasure Island.*

The next morning, Dad asked a deputy sheriff to stop by so he could ask him some questions; Dad didn't want to disturb the mound of rocks if it was a grave. The Sheriff's Office said to go ahead, so we removed the stones by hand, and when we did, we found nothing but an empty hole. Dennis was sure it had been constructed as a grave for an Indian chief, Dad was sure it once held a pot full of gold. I was just glad it didn't hold a skeleton.

— 4 —

IN EARLY AUGUST, we received one of those telephone calls you hope you never have to answer; Great Grandpa had died in his sleep. He was eighty-nine years old. I don't remember there being much grieving, except by Dennis, maybe it was because he had lived a long, full life, or in the chaos, taking place as Mom and Dad tried to prepare for a quick trip to Southern California, there wasn't time. Our 1962 Chrysler needed new tires and an oil change, there were contractors who needed to be called so their jobs could be moved back a week or cancelled. Dad also had to make out schedules and paychecks. With both Dad and Grandpa leaving, the business shut down, except for a few men who were left to take calls and do odd jobs around the plant.

Mom had arranged for our aunt to stay with us for the week. Frantically, she rushed to town to get groceries, washed and dried every bit of laundry, and packed for both herself and Dad. They kissed us good-bye early the next morning, and along with Grandpa, Grandma, and an assorted group of family members, they departed as a caravan for Southern California.

It would be a twenty-four-hour trip with no planned stops, other than to eat and buy gas. A sullen-faced Dennis joined his parents in their car; it was a lonely week without Mom and Dad and Dennis. There were no rides with Dad, no days with Dennis running the rock crusher or playing catch, but mostly during this week, I missed Mom. I had never previously considered all she did for us, and our aunt was a terrible cook!

They had no problems for the first part of the trip, but as they passed through Redding, California, the temperature began to soar as the California sun beat down through the windows of the overcrowded Chrysler. They had the windows down to allow the breeze to blow through the car, but with no air-conditioning everyone was sweltering, especially my mom, who had a tendency to get overheated. The temperature had climbed to over 104 degrees, Mom had stopped sweating and her face and arms had become beet red. Dad quickly recognized if they didn't get her cooled down immediately, she might go into shock from heat stroke. They were able to find a public swimming pool, and with ice packs and plenty of liquids, they got her body temperature back to normal. They stayed there until early evening before proceeding south again. This time, they took a cooler full of ice and water along with them, and several washcloths to cool themselves off as they traveled. They reached Banning, California, the next day, found local accommodations, checked in, and tried to rest. The funeral was scheduled for 10:00 a.m. the next morning.

In the evening as they sat and ate dinner together, the atmosphere relaxed a little, as the pressure of making it to the funeral on time passed. Grandpa and Grandma announced they were going to stay in Banning after the funeral for a week or so, and would take the train home.

The family discussion then turned to when should the caravan of relatives return home, and what did they want to do before they left. A consensus was reached; they agreed they would stay for three more days after the funeral, so they could visit with the relatives who lived in Palm Springs and the Los Angeles area. They also made plans to spend a day at Disneyland and Knox Berry Farms. More importantly, they agreed to take the coast route home to avoid the heat they had endured on their southbound journey. Their return plan included stops in San Francisco and the Redwood Forrest.

The trip home was a life-altering experience for Dennis; completely mesmerized with the San Francisco Bay area, and the Northern California coast, it was all he talked about. He told me he planned to hitchhike back there as soon as possible. My sisters and I just wanted to know about

Disneyland, what were the rides like, did he see Mickey Mouse, and it's a Small World.

With Mom, Dad, and Dennis back home, life soon returned to normal. Dad and Dennis went to work each day and my sisters and I continued our summer vacations. Blackberry-picking season had arrived and each day, I awoke early and raced to be first at the best spots. In the afternoon, Mom would drive me into town to the feed store to turn in my flats of berries. The going rate was two dollars a flat, I could pick two flats a day, and the season usually lasted about three weeks. I figured if I picked berries for six days a week for three weeks, I could make seventy dollars or more. With the money, I could help buy my own school clothes, maybe a new baseball glove, and a few fishing lures. I remember Dennis telling me I needed to buy Levi's Blue Jeans and black Converse high tops.

"They're what the cool kids wear," he said.

Mom let me buy the shoes, but not the jeans.

She said, "There is no reason to spend so much money on jeans you will grow out of before Christmas."

On my birthday, Mom dropped my sisters and me off at Grandma's for the afternoon because she needed to go grocery shopping. I knew the shopping also included buying my birthday present. I really hadn't asked for anything special, but the anticipation of what I might get grew stronger with each passing hour. By the time she returned, Grandma had made rhubarb pie, she put ten candles on it, and I blew them out. I hate rhubarb pie, but being polite, I graciously ate it. At least she had root beer, my favorite soda pop. After I finished my pie, Grandma gave me my present. As fast I could, I tore off the wrapping, uncovering a brand-new fishing pole with a spinning reel. When I looked at her face, I could see in her eyes as much joy as I was feeling. I told her I loved it, and I gave her a big hug. She told me happy birthday.

My old fishing pole had belonged to my uncle, and it didn't have a reel. I fished by throwing the weight and hook out into the river, and when I got a bite, I'd run up the bank and pull in the fish. But with my new pole and reel, I could fish like a real fisherman.

While we were still visiting at Grandma's, the phone rang. I could see the concern on my mom's face as she spoke, but I couldn't tell who she was speaking to. When she finished talking, she just smiled, and said we needed to get going; we still have many things to do today.

On the way home, I didn't talk, and if others did, I didn't hear them; my thoughts were focused on my new fishing pole, and all the fish I was going to catch.

When we pulled into our driveway, I could see a banner hanging in the carport that said "Happy Birthday," and underneath the banner sat a dog with his tongue out and his curled tail wagging. I recognized him as the dog I'd seen in the newspaper. My mom looked very surprised, the phone call she had received at Grandma's was from my Father who said Champ had gotten loose from his chain and had run away.

Overwhelmed with excitement at the sight of Champ, I began to cry. If there was ever a dog created for a ten-year-old boy, there was never one better than Champ!

As I held him and stroked his glistening coat, he licked my face. Dad came out of the house and said, "He came back on his own; as if he knew he belonged here, and he needed to be here to greet someone special."

Everyone said happy birthday and we all went inside, including Champ. I started crying again as I hugged Mom and Dad, and told them I loved them so much.

They smiled, and told me, "Every young boy deserves a dog of his own."

Later, they told me the whole story, about how Dad had told Mom about me seeing Champ in the newspaper, and how they talked about it and decided I should have my own dog. They called to see if Champ was still available and the animal shelter said yes, so after dropping us off at Grandma's they went to pick him up.

Their story about leaving the animal shelter was even more amazing. As soon as they were out the door, Champ slipped out his collar and took off across the parking lot. As they watched, he crossed the street, and jumped into the back of a blue station wagon through the open back window.

My parents said, "We just stood there in amazement, he had just jumped into the back of our car."

We tried to keep Champ on a chain for the next few days, but each time, he'd just shake his head until he wiggled out the collar. We gave up and no longer attempted to keep him on a chain. Champ became my constant companion and my best friend.

Labor Day came and went, and I began school again. Dennis continued to work for Dad, then one day, Aunt Sarah, Dennis's mother, called to tell him he had received an official letter from the Draft Board.

By Sunday, everyone knew about it, the pastor even said a special prayer for Dennis. The next day, he reported to the local recruiting office and was sworn in. A week later, Dennis packed up his things, and moved back to his parent's home. From that point forward, things weren't the same, school had restarted, Dennis no longer worked for Dad, and I was spending most of my free time fishing or playing with Champ.

The summer was officially over.

Dennis had saved his money all summer, and he had about three weeks before he had to report for induction. A couple of his school friends had also received their draft notices as well, and Dennis convinced them to join him and hitchhike to San Francisco. We saw each other one last time at church before he left for boot camp.

I asked him if he took any pictures of San Francisco, he said, "All my pictures are in my head. Did you know our minds record everything we see and do! Along with the images, our minds also record the emotional experience, the sounds, the smells, the taste, we don't need photographs, all we have to do is recall the experiences from our mind, and we can relive them again and again."

"Have you ever heard someone say, the experience left me with a bad taste in my mouth? The mind records everything."

As we parted, he gave me a hug, we wouldn't see each other until he came back home on leave for Christmas.

I wasn't sure what Dennis's future experiences were going to be like, but the experience of saying good-bye, left a bad taste in my mouth.

− 5 −

Between Summers One and Two

ENNIS RETURNED FOR Christmas, but he only had two weeks before he had to leave again. On New Year's Day, his parents had a special going away potluck for him. Grandpa and Grandma gave him a Bible, Dad told him to find good Christian friends, and don't volunteer for anything. It was common to have potlucks in our family, but they had always in the past been about happy events. Today seemed very solemn, like someone had died.

At the end of the afternoon, everyone lined up to say good-bye to Dennis. I got in line, and when my turn arrived, he picked me up and gave me a bear hug. I asked him if he would be back by next summer so he could live with us again. He said, "Maybe." But I knew his "maybe" meant no.

On the way home, I asked my mother why everyone was so sad.

She said, "Dennis is in the army now, and would soon be headed to Vietnam to fight in the war, and we wouldn't see him for at least a year or more."

I didn't talk the rest of the way home, neither did anyone else. Dad didn't even turn the radio on. I sat and looked out the window and tried to recall the pictures I had stored up in my mind about Dennis.

The next summer passed without Dennis, but life continued. I went swimming, rode my new bike, played little league for the first time, picked blackberries, and of course, played with Champ, my constant companion, except during baseball. I helped one of Dad's employees run the rock crusher but it wasn't as much fun as the previous summer. He didn't play the radio, or sing along with every Beach Boys' song.

Dennis got two weeks leave during Christmas of 1966, but he didn't come home. Instead, he chose to hitchhike around Germany with a couple of his buddies. He did send me a postcard from Munich; it was a picture of a nightclub called the Cave, the note on the back said, "It's where the Beatles were discovered." I hung it up on the wall next to my bed.

What I couldn't understand was why he would choose to spend Christmas with friends instead of with his family and those who loved him.

As the fall of 1967 approached, everyone was anticipating Dennis's return. When he did return, the family threw him a big party. Everyone wanted to know what his future plans were. I just wanted to play catch and share about little league.

"Last year, I had played outfield, but this year, I played short stop," I said. "I hadn't hit any home runs yet, but I had stolen lots of bases."

I wanted him to come home with us, I hoped he would stay for a couple days. *It would be like old times,* I thought. He never did.

I felt like I must have done something wrong to make him not want to play with me.

I expected to see him at church on Sundays, but he never showed up. I heard he had tried to find a job but was having a hard time finding one. Then I heard he had re-enlisted, the army had promised him a bonus and a chef's position at a base in Germany. I wondered if he'd be making peanut butter, coconut, chocolate-chip pancakes for the troops. A few weeks later, Dennis flew to Germany.

Dad said, "This time, he would learn a trade he could use, and he isn't in Vietnam carrying a gun anymore."

Others said, "Dennis needed the change, he had become moody and impatient. He had always been a boy who couldn't sit still, but now he seemed more restless than before."

I also had overheard Dennis had been seen drinking at local bars, and he had told Austin he regularly used pot. I'm not sure if Dennis was bored, or trying to escape, but once again, he had vanished.

During his second tour of duty, Dennis did come home for one Thanksgiving. My parents had built a new house, and all the relatives were invited for Thanksgiving dinner. Dennis and I, along with the other men, spent most of the afternoon watching the Dallas Cowboys play the Detroit Lions on TV. When the game ended, we strutted outside and had our own game of touch football. It had been three years since Dennis and I played baseball in the backyard, I was now thirteen, eight inches taller, and at least forty pounds heavier, and I came up to nearly his chin.

My father and Austin chose teams. I was on Dad's team, he played quarterback, and I played a receiver. On the first play, Dad called a fly route, and I caught his pass for a touchdown. From then on, the other team respected me, and covered me more closely. Dennis scored three touchdowns for his team; once he got into the open, no one could catch him. We played until the old men were pooped out, and then a few us continued a while longer. In the end, Dennis and I were the only ones left and we just played catch. It was like old times in the backyard once again.

I shared with Dennis about my baptism the previous summer. I said, "The river was so cold that when the pastor dunked me, it took my breath away."

He said, "I remember doing that when I was about your age."

When Dennis finally got out of the army for the second time, he decided to travel for a while before he'd get a job. He had no commitments, he had saved his pay from the army, and he had a desire to see America. He got up one morning, walked out to the highway, stuck his thumb out, and caught a ride south toward San Francisco. I don't know everywhere he visited, or everything he did, but I know he spent time in San Francisco and Denver and places in between during his travels. One of those places was a small town near Denver called Loveland. His best friend from his time in Germany had recently got out of the army as well. They hung out for a few weeks before Dennis headed back home.

For whatever reason, it could have been the war, or maybe his choice of lifestyle, but Dennis became a recluse. He avoided family and friends, and kept to himself, preferring to be on his own. For the next few years, he wandered up and down the Pacific Coast from Northern California to Washington, working as a chef. He worked at some very renowned restaurants as well as some insignificant holes in the wall, but he never seemed to stay anywhere for very long. He would tell me later he loved cooking seafood and the ocean. There's nothing like waking up to the sound of waves crashing, and the smell of sea salt. Starting your day off with a walk on the beach, with the ocean spray in your face, lets you know you're still alive.

In 1972, I heard Dennis had gotten married to a young woman from Coos Bay, Oregon. She was a server at the place he worked. He brought her up to meet his parents, but there had been no formal introduction to the rest of the family. The marriage didn't last a year before she filed for divorce. The next thing I heard, he was working in Long Beach, Washington, at a seafood bar and grill. After I got my driver's license, I asked my parents if I could drive to the beach with my cousin Austin to see Dennis. They said yes, but not to stay too late, they didn't want me driving on the windy roads after dark. So Austin and I left early and got there a little after 10:00 a.m.

We stopped by the place Dennis worked at, but they said he didn't usually come in until noon, but he lived just around the corner. So we walked to his place and knocked on the door. It took a while, but Dennis finally came to the door and opened it. At first, by the look on his face, I wasn't sure if he recognized us. He was half-awake at best and obviously had been drinking the night before. But after a few seconds, his brain woke up, and a big smile came across his face and he welcomed us in.

His place had no place to sit, he had only a bed and an old TV, and there were no chairs or a table. So we stood and talked. It felt very uncomfortable, I felt like we were invading his personal space, and I thought to myself, *Why is he living like this, what does he do with his money, he had a better place to live the summer he lived in my parent's unfinished addition.* We visited for maybe an hour before Dennis said, "I need to get ready for work."

Before we left, Austin told Dennis they were hiring at the boat factory, where he worked, and he said, "You can stay with me until you can get your own place, if you want."

Dennis said, "I'll think about it," and we left.

A week later, Dennis called Austin, and a few days later, Dennis returned to Longview and began working at the boat factory. He stayed with Austin a few weeks before getting a place of his own. Dennis also started to come around to family gatherings during the holidays again, but he never came to church.

I thought maybe the war was finally over for him, or at least, the war with himself. I saw it as the opportunity to renew the friendship of the older brother I had lost.

– 6 –

The Second Summer 1974

THE WEEK BEFORE high school graduation, my cousin
Austin told me there was a summer job for me at the
boat factory where he and Dennis worked, if I wanted
it. It sounded like the perfect fit; I could earn some extra
money before going off to college in the fall, and I would
be working alongside Austin and Dennis.

My initial college dream was to play football for
Washington State University, but they weren't offering
me a football scholarship, being 5'10" tall, weighing 140
pounds, and being slower than most college linemen might
have had something to do with it. So I turned to my second
dream, to play professional golf. The college I had chosen
had a golf team, but no scholarships, just free golf, and the
opportunity to play against high quality, nationally ranked
players. I hadn't even decided what I would study, maybe

business or accounting, I thought, but thanks to my high school counselor, who helped me fill out the paperwork, I had a Pell Grant to cover the cost of my room and board, books, and tuition.

I hoped working with Austin and Dennis would be something like the summer Dennis and I had worked together years ago. So I accepted the job. I graduated on Friday night and started working at the boat factory on Monday morning.

The first week at work was all about being initiated. Besides myself, there were two other recent high school graduates hired. We were assigned to work in the paint shop. My first initiation experience took me completely by surprise—a man who worked in the paint shop, came over to welcome me aboard. He shook my hand and we began talking, Dennis and Austin joined us, soon my pants leg began to feel wet. I looked down and to my shock, it looked like he was peeing on me! This was the first of many pranks and jokes I would have to endure.

The truth is, he had cut a finger off a pink Playtex glove, poked a hole in the end of the finger, and then attached the finger to a water bottle with duct tape. Next, he carefully placed the bottle into his front overall's pocket with the finger protruding from his crotch, and with just a little squeeze on water bottle, it looked like you were being peed on.

The other trick they liked to play on rookies was to tape a full Playtex glove to an air hose, then slide it into your work area. They then turned the air on. The Playtex glove would fill-up like a balloon; it would grow to about the size of a large hog, and then explode. The first time it happened to me, I jumped a good three feet into the air and spun around, only to see several men, including Dennis, laughing their heads off. By the end of the week, I was so jumpy, even the smallest noise would cause me to freak out.

After a few weeks, the pranks subsided. The others and I were now considered part of the crew, and were expected to start completing our share of the workload. Austin trained me to paste wallpaper to the walls of several of the different yachts. I enjoyed working at the same place as my cousins; the place was like an extended family, and the place had a jovial atmosphere, even if some days, it felt like you were working at a target gallery, and you were the target. Each day, I learned something new, and it didn't take long to realize the low man on the totem pole gets all the dirty jobs. Sanding the underbelly of the boats was the worst. To protect the hull, everything below the waterline had to be sanded and then painted. The hulls of the boats were made of fiberglass. You had to get into an outfit that looked like a cheap space suit, to protect yourself from airborne particles of fiberglass that covered everything once you started sanding. One boat could take several days, and you sweated like a pig inside the suit, and even when you took the suit off, your nose was plugged, and the corners of your eyes were caked from the fine fiberglass dust. The good news was that after sanding and painting all the available hulls, I got a dollar-an-hour raise. I now made a staggering thirty-two dollars a day.

The summer months are always the busiest manufacturing months at the boat factory. At any given time, there are eight to ten yachts being assembled. The "Third Quarter" is also the company's most profitable quarter economically as well. This makes the summer months the most susceptible months to union strikes. In the never-ending tug of war between the union and the company, I found myself in the middle of the next battle. Negotiators from the union and the company had failed to reach an agreement before the previous contract elapsed at the end of July, and now, three weeks later, with no further talks scheduled, it appeared a strike was inevitable.

On August 20, the union voted to strike, and by the next day, the employees had picket lines in place, one in front of the factory, and another in front of the company headquarters. As a temporary employee, I wasn't eligible for strike pay. Nor did I have any vacation time available like Dennis and Austin, so I had no recourse but to wait for the strike to end. College classes started in about a month, and there wasn't really enough time to find another full-time job, so I decided to wait and see what would happen. I hung around the house the first day of the strike, and played golf on the second day with Austin and Dennis.

As we teed-up on the first hole, Dennis said, "I'm going to take my two weeks of paid vacation if the strike doesn't end by the end of the week."

Austin said, "I've got three week's vacation pay coming, but I think I'm going to hold on to it for a while. I'm scheduled to be on the picket line the next two days, so I'll get more of the scuttlebutt, and then decide."

All Union workers had to take their turn on the line, unless they were on vacation. In exchange for walking the picket line, they were paid strike, which amounted to a few dollars a day.

As we completed the first nine holes and started the back nine, I asked Dennis what he planned to do on his vacation. One conversation led to another, and by the end of our round of golf, Dennis and I had made plans to hitch-hike to San Francisco and maybe farther.

When I told my parents my plans, I wouldn't say they were thrilled, but they didn't try to dissuade me. I told them I would call them every other day, and we would call Austin every day, and if the strike ended, we would catch a Greyhound bus home immediately.

My Pell Grant covered my college cost for the year, and I had saved nearly all of the money I had earned during the summer, so I was financially capable. They didn't disagree.

Dad shrugged his shoulders and said, "Just be careful, and take enough money for an extra couple of days worth of meals and a bus ticket home."

As we made plans to leave, I asked Dennis for a list of items I needed. Dennis was an expert, he had made this trip several times, as well as many others, so I relied upon his knowledge to help me prepare.

He gave me a list of items to bring: a hooded sweat-shirt, three T-shirts, three pairs of underwear, two pair of jeans, one pair of shorts, a pocket knife, six pairs of socks, a good pair of shoes, a four-foot-by-eight-foot tarp, a six-foot-long piece of rope, a lighter, sun glasses, suntan lotion, a deck of playing cards, a bar of soap, razor, a stocking cap, a roll of toilet paper, a towel, deodorant, money for two meals a day, a hundred dollars for two nights' stay in San Francisco, plus an extra hundred for emergencies and the bus fare home. Dennis also gave me a short list of things to do before we left: get your hair cut short, get a tetanus shot, and practice packing all your supplies several times.

He gave specific instructions of how to pack: take the tarp and fold it in half, so it is two feet by eight feet, then take your stocking cap and put the lotion, soap, deodorant, and toilet paper in it. Then place the full stocking cap into the hood of the sweatshirt. Next, take your unrolled towel and place all the clothing you're not wearing in it, and then roll the towel up. Place the towel inside the shirt part of the hooded sweatshirt and roll it up. Lastly, place the rolled-up hooded sweatshirt in the once-folded tarp, and roll the tarp up. Secure the tarp with the piece of rope, and make sure to make a loop in the rope for a handle. The other items not packed, you will keep in your pants pockets. When the tarp is tied up, it should be size of a thin sleeping bag.

After going through the list of items to bring and how to pack them, Dennis shared the five rules of hitchhiking with me. Rule Number One: always have short hair, be clean-shaven, and wear clean clothes, most people won't pick up hippies and bums. Rule Number Two: don't carry too much; people don't want to open their trunks, they expect you to hold whatever you have on your lap. Rule Number Three: keep the conversation focused on them; people like to talk about themselves and what they know, so ask their advice about the local spots to eat, the best places to camp, and about the local history. Rule Number Four: any ride is better than walking, so smile when you stick out your thumb, and act as if you're having fun. Rule Number Five: the best ride is always with pretty girls!

The next couple of days pasted slowly as my excitement about the trip grew with each time I thought about the upcoming adventure. On Friday, Dennis checked with the union leadership about the status of the negotiations. With no settlement in sight, he applied for paid vacation time with the company. Dennis called about noon to say we would leave the next morning around 8:00 a.m. The last thing he said was to wear two pairs of socks, "You don't want blisters."

I couldn't sleep at all; it was like waiting for the first day of school to arrive. I got up early, had a bowl of cereal, and told my parents I loved them before I left. I put my rolled-up belongings in my car and headed for Dennis's apartment building. When I got there, the front door was open, and Dennis was waiting. He asked, "Are you ready?" I used the restroom and then we started off on our journey. We walked the couple of blocks to Oregon Way Boulevard, which led to the Rainer Bridge, which crosses the Columbia River. As soon as we hit Oregon Way, we began hitchhiking. Dennis told me to take the lead, and he would follow me with his thumb out. We caught a ride from one of the first cars coming by. The man gave us the short ride across the bridge to Oregon where he dropped us off. From the bridge, the highway to the coast begins with a steep climb. For nearly two miles, near the top, is a popular viewpoint travelers stop at to take pictures of Mount St. Helens. Dennis said we'd be able to catch our next ride from there.

When we reached the viewpoint, there were no cars there, so we took a few minutes to rest. As we viewed the white coned-shaped Cascade Mountain peak in the distance, Dennis asked if I knew the Indian legend about Mount St. Helens. I quickly learned Dennis would be more than a traveling companion on this trip; he would also be a tour guide with an exceptional knowledge of history and geography.

Dennis said, "According to the legend, a great spirit named Tyhee Sahale, along with his two sons, traveled down the mighty Columbia River in search of a new home for their people. When they reached the present day area of the Dalles, Oregon, Sahale decided this would be their new home. As the boys reached manhood, they began to quarrel over the leadership of the tribe. Sahale, not wanting to see his sons fight, decided they should both be chiefs, so he took out his bow and shot one arrow to the north, across the Columbia River, and a second arrow to the west. He then instructed each son to take those members of the tribe who wished to follow, and go find their arrow. The son, and the members of the tribe who went north with him, would become known as the Klickitats. The son, and members of the tribe who went west, would become known as the Multnomahs. Sahale wanted the two new tribes to interact with each other, so as a sign of peace between the two tribes, Sahale created a stone bridge across the Columbia River, and the people called it the Bridge of the Gods. Its location was near the present day city of Stevenson, Washington.

"As the tribes grew in size, they became evil and jealous of each other, and they began to quarrel with one another. This displeased Sahale. So he covered the sun and the people began to freeze. Another Great Spirit named Loo-wit saw the people suffering and took pity on them; she went to Sahale and offered to share her gift of fire with them. Sahale agreed to allow this, and the leaders from the tribes met at the bridge where Loo-wit gave each tribe the knowledge of fire. In exchange for sharing her gift, Sahale changed Loo-wit into a beautiful maiden with eternal youth and beauty.

"Now the chiefs from both tribes fell in love with Loo-wit, and both chiefs asked for her hand in marriage, but she refused to give either an answer. Soon Loo-wit's failure to choose caused both tribes to war against each other, and blood was shed. This made Sahale very angry. First, he destroyed the Bridge of the Gods so the tribes could not destroy each other, then he turned Loo-wit and his two sons into mountains. When the first white settlers arrived, they gave the mountains the names, Mount St. Helens, Mount Adams, and Mount Hood. It is said, even today, Loo-wit is the envy of all mountains because of her exceptional beauty."

After finishing his story, Dennis asked, "What are you hoping to get out of this trip?"

I said, "To see the sights, to experience a little of the nomadic, carefree lifestyle, and spend some time with you. What about you, what are you hoping for?"

"I'm looking forward to revisiting places I haven't seen for a few years, and renewing some old friendships."

We were at the viewpoint for only about fifteen minutes before a red Oldsmobile Cutlass pulled into the parking lot. A young couple got out and stretched a bit. He was wearing bell-bottom jeans and a white T-shirt. She was wearing a pale-yellow blouse and a white mini-skirt. He took his camera out and had her pose with Mount St. Helens in the background as he snapped a few pictures. As they started to leave, Dennis stuck out his thumb. They pulled up next to us, and asked where we were headed. Dennis said, "South."

The man gave us the once-over slowly before he said, "We're going as far as Seaside if you want a ride."

After settling into the backseat, Dennis introduced us. He said, "I'm Dennis, and this is Nathan."

The man looked at the woman, and then replied, "I'm Mike and this is my wife Kelli. We got married a year ago, and we're on our way to Seaside, Oregon, to celebrate our wedding anniversary."

I said, "I'm from Woodland and Dennis is from Longview, and we're hitchhiking to San Francisco."

Remembering Rule Number Three, I asked where they were from, how they liked their car, had they been to Seaside before. I stopped asking any further questions because they all seemed to be so contrived. After a short lull in the conversation, Dennis asked if they had been to Fort Clatsop, which is near Seaside.

"It's a replica of the original fort Lewis and Clark constructed during their expedition," Dennis said, "It's named after the Clatsop Indians who inhabited the area and befriended Lewis and Clark and their men during the winter they spent at the mouth of the Columbia River. Today, besides the replica of the fort, there's also an interpretive center and museum at the site."

Kelli said, "I haven't, but it sounds like a great place to visit. I teach fourth grade, and Lewis and Clark are a part of my social studies curriculum."

While Kelli had not been to the fort, she did know the beach at Seaside is where the expedition had boiled saltwater to get salt for curing the elk meat they would need for their return trip home.

After Kelli shared about the salt making, Dennis shared more about the Lewis and Clark expedition.

He said, "Originally, the expedition had settled on the Washington State side of the Columbia River on the Long Beach Peninsula because they hoped to meet a sailing ship and send word back to President Jefferson they were alive and safe. But after several weeks of constant rain with no shelter and no ships in sight, Lewis and Clark convened a meeting of the men to decide whether they should move or not.

"The expedition felt the Chinook Indians who inhabited the area charged exorbitant prices for food and supplies, and stole everything not nailed down or guarded when they weren't looking. The men hated fish and preferred elk meat, which was in abundance on the Oregon side of the river, and even though it meant giving up their chances of meeting a ship, they voted to move."

Mike said, "That's very interesting, did you know that, Kelli?"

"I didn't," she said, "But I do know several of the Chinook Indian legends. I always share a few each year with my class when we study Pacific Northwest Native Americans. My favorite is the raven and the man who sits on the tides.

"One day the Raven, the smartest of all birds, was walking along the shoreline, hunting for food, when he thought to himself, *If I could somehow get the ocean to recede each day for just a short time, I could find all the food I'd ever need.* So the Raven began asking other birds if they knew how to make the ocean recede. He asked the gulls, but they didn't know. So he asked the gray pelicans, but they didn't know. They suggested he ask the sandpipers, but he couldn't catch them as they ran here and there as a group of hundreds with a single mind.

"About to give up, he asked the albatrosses, who said, 'Go ask the Fog Man.'

"The Raven asked, 'Where can I find this Fog Man?' and the albatrosses said, 'Fly north and you will find him.' So the Raven flew north until he spotted a man the size of an island floating in the ocean.

"He swooped down to talk to the man, but the man said, 'Go away, and leave me alone.' The man then put on his hat, the fog began to roll out of his hat, and soon the Raven could not see at all because the fog was so thick. The Raven, being extremely intelligent, decided to wait, and when the fog cleared, he asked the man, 'How can I make the ocean recede?'

"The Fog Man reached for his hat again, but before he could reach it, the Raven stole it from him. The Fog Man said, 'I don't know, but the man who sits on the tides would know, now can I have my hat back?'

"But the Raven said, 'Not until you tell me where I can find the Man Who Sits on the Tides.' After the Fog Man gave him the information, the Raven flew off with his hat anyway.

"The Raven next flew straight into the setting sun for hours, until he saw a giant of a man sitting in the ocean. The Raven flew down to speak to him; the Raven said to the Giant, 'Do you know how to make the ocean recede?' To which the Giant responded, 'No, I'm the Man who sits on the Tides, it's who I am, it's what I do, it's what I've always done.'

"The Raven then asked the Giant what would happen if he stood up. The Giant responded, 'I don't know, I'm the Man who sits on the Tides, it's who I am, it's what I do, it's what I've always done.'

"The Raven thought about it for a while, and then he flew high into the sky, and then plummeting down, he struck the Giant like an arrow in the back. The Giant stood up in pain, and when he did, the ocean began to rush into the hole where he once sat. The ocean then receded from the seashore, and all the birds and other animals feasted on the food now left uncovered. But after the pain wore off, the Giant once again sat down, causing the ocean to return to its normal height. So the Raven once again flew out to the Giant, but the Giant saw him coming, and began swatting at him with his mighty hands, so the Raven put on the Fog Man's hat, and when the Giant could no longer see, the Raven struck him again. The Giant stood up once again in pain. From that day forward, the Raven made two trips a day out to the Giant. Then one day, as he approached, the Giant on his own stood up, and stretched, causing the ocean to recede. The Raven asked the Giant why he did that, to which the Giant replied, 'I am The Man who causes the tides. It's who I am, it's what I do, it's what I've always done.' From that day forward, the Raven has always been able to eat twice a day each time the tide recedes."

Soon after Kelli finished her story, we arrived at Seaside. We thanked them for the ride, and they wished us safe travel. We started walking south along Highway 101, as we waited for our next ride; Dennis said, "Shall we play a game?"

"The way it's played," he said, "Is one player asks the question, the other player gives an answer, then the first player gives their answer, then you argue over who's right. It's called The Greatest Game."

"I remember this game," I said, "You taught it to me the summer you worked for Grandpa and Dad."

Dennis's question was, "Who was greatest NFL quarterback of all time?"

I said, "That's easy, Joe Willie Namath. No one has ever been better than him."

Dennis said, "No, the greatest NFL quarterback was Johnny Unitas."

"How can you say that?" I said. "They played against each other in the greatest NFL game ever played, the 1969 Super Bowl, and the Colts lost."

"No, you're wrong," Dennis said, "Unitas didn't play in the Super Bowl game. His back-up Earl Morrall did."

"I still say Namath is the greatest. He was the first quarterback to throw for over four thousand yards in a season, and he single-handedly elevated the lowly American Football League to a point where they became legitimate rivals to the National Football league."

"Namath was more hype than stature," Dennis said, "Who ever heard of a quarterback being called Broadway? Just look at the stats, Johnny Unitas played for seventeen years, won two World Championships. He passed for over forty thousand yards and 290 touchdowns. He was chosen for ten Pro-Bowls and as the League MVP three times. No one else even comes close."

I said, "If you couldn't choose either Namath or Unitas, who would you choose?"

Dennis said, "I'd pick Bart Starr."

"Yeah," I said, "or maybe Fran Tarkenton."

I said, "Have you ever heard the story about Joe Namath and where he lived when he attended the University of Alabama? When Joe was recruited to play football at Alabama, Coach Bear Bryant arranged for him to stay at a home owned by a wealthy older lady.

"One day the woman said to Joe, 'Take off my shoes, Joe. Now take off my pearls, Joe.

"'Joe, please take off my gloves. Now, Joe, I need you to unzip my dress and take it off!

"Then she said, 'You listen to me, young man, this is the last time, I'm going to tell you to quit wearing my jewelry and clothes.'"

"Where did you hear that?" Dennis said.

"It's in his book, the story gets everybody every time," I said.

We hadn't walked for maybe more than a mile when we got another ride. A blue Crew Crummy, the kind used by logging companies to haul their employees back and forth to their worksites, pulled over and offered us a ride. The driver said he was headed to Coos Bay and asked if we wanted a ride. We said yes, we had hit the jackpot. This ride would take us a couple of hundred miles. The driver's name was Russ, and he was a big man, probably 6'5" and weighed at least 280 pounds. He had a big chew of tobacco in his mouth and swore about every fourth word. He had on a flannel shirt with the sleeves cut off, and it was buttoned only halfway up. He had to be the hairiest man I'd ever seen. I started to think maybe Russ was related to Sasquatch, the mythical Big Foot who roams the woods of the Pacific Northwest. I tried to get a look at his feet, but Dennis's legs were in the way.

Russ was definitely colorful. I asked him who he thought was the greatest NFL quarterback. He said, "Sonny Jorgensen." I knew from his choice this wasn't a person I wanted to debate with.

The Crummy smelled like gas and oil from the four chainsaws stored in the back. I ignored the smell the best I could, remembering Rule Number Four: any ride is better than walking. Russ entertained us the whole trip with his jokes and stories. As we traveled, Russ pointed out places that still showed the scars from the Tillamook Burn. A series of devastating wildfires that besieged the area between 1933 and 1951 destroying over three hundred and fifty thousand acres of old-growth forest.

Dennis shared, "The fire which began in 1945 is believed by many to have been started by one of the incendiary balloons launched by the Japanese during World War II. The balloons were designed to catch the high-altitude jet stream, cross the Pacific Ocean, and set fires along the West Coast of the United States."

"Several of the balloons reached our coastline," Dennis said. "But there is no concrete evidence any of them actually accomplished their mission."

On the south side of the city of Tillamook, Russ pointed out the World War II Naval Air Base. Russ said, "The base housed blimps during the war that were used to spot Japanese submarines. The two huge hangars are made totally of wood and are believed to be the largest wood structures in the world."

After Russ stopped for gas in Newport, I fell asleep, only to be awakened by a jab in the ribs from Dennis who accused me of snoring so loud that Russ thought there was something wrong with the vehicle. An hour later, when I fell asleep again, I awoke to the slamming of brakes and both Dennis and Russ screaming. They began laughing hysterically as my arms flailed around trying to brace myself for what I believed must be an impending impact. After regaining my senses, I laughed along with them as they recounted the look on my face repeatedly. I promised myself to never fall asleep again during one of our rides.

As we continued our progress south on Highway 101 toward Coos Bay, we passed through Florence, Oregon.

Russ informed us this is where he grew up and where most of his family still lives. He told us Florence is a small coastal community where the economy is based mostly on logging, commercial fishing, and summer tourism.

Russ said, "It had its fifteen minutes of fame back in 1970 when local officials decided to explode a large dead gray whale which had washed up on the local beach. It wasn't the first time a dead whale had washed ashore along the Pacific Coast, but it was the first time one had ever been exploded. Usually, the dead whale is buried or pushed back into the ocean, then tied to a boat and carried miles out to sea where it is left to become food for the creatures of the sea. But this time, several attempts to push the whale back into the sea had failed, so someone conceived the idea of exploding the whale with dynamite. The belief was the whale would be blown into millions of small pieces, the seabirds, crabs, and other assorted carnivores would then devour the remains or they would be washed out to sea."

"When the day came for the big event, people from all over the area came to witness it, reporters from all three major news networks from Portland showed up to film it, much to the locals' dismay."

Russ continued, "They cordoned off the area to keep onlookers from getting too close. Me and several family members watched from the roof of a nearby home. When the whale exploded, all you could see was this large cloud of sand, blood, water, blubber, and whale guts fly into the sky. Seconds later, the same began to fall to the earth. Those who had gathered as close as they could found themselves covered in the fallout. A large chunk of the whale came down on the roof of a visitor's car, destroying it. We watched it all," Russ said. "And then we watched it again on the five o'clock news.

"It reminded me of the movie *Butch Cassidy and the Sundance Kid*, where they're blowing up the safe from the train. The explosion sends the money flying everywhere, to which Sundance says to Butch, 'You might have used a little too much dynamite there Butch!'"

After an hour in the Crummy, I'd gotten used to the gas smell and dismissed the idea Russ might be related to Sasquatch. Russ was a classic case of learning to not judge a book by its cover; I kept that in mind throughout the rest of our trip.

We got to Coos Bay in the late afternoon; Russ dropped us off at a local restaurant he recommended. I thanked him for the ride. Dennis shook his hand, as if he was saying good-bye to his best friend. Russ had a way of tickling Dennis's funny bone; they had laughed nearly the whole time, much of the time at me.

We had dinner, bought a newspaper, and then made our way to the beach. The wind was blowing intermittently, so the first thing we did was locate some shelter. We found a large tangled piece of driftwood and began settling in for the evening, out of the wind. Next, we gathered wood to start a fire, using twigs, dried grass, and some of the newspaper we'd bought. We had the fire going in no time. We then added larger pieces of wood until we had a nice fire that would last all night long. We unrolled our tarps and placed them down on the ground as a barrier between the moist sand and ourselves. The wind began to die down as the daylight waned. A surreal feeling overtook me as I watched the waves roll to the shore then back out again in a rhythmic motion while feeling the warmth of the crackling fire. We just sat and relaxed. There is something about a fire, especially at night, I'm not sure what makes it so enchanting, but I can just stare at it for hours. It's hypnotic, kind of like watching television. It reminded me of the fires we had at our secret campsite. As the sunset and the stars began to shine, you could see a few other campfires glowing up and down the beach.

Dennis said, "This was one of my favorite things about hitchhiking along the Pacific Coast, the beach belongs to everyone, and it's a great place to stay during the summer time. Most have public access, a restroom with running water, and best of all, it's a free place to stay."

The topic of conversation this evening was politics. I asked Dennis if he thought the president was guilty. Having been only a few weeks since President Nixon had resigned the presidency instead of facing impeachment from what has become known as the Watergate Scandal.

Dennis said, "He thought the whole affair, which was played out like a daily afternoon soap opera on TV, was a witch hunt by the democrats until they played the tapes with erased sections." He said, "Even if Nixon wasn't part of the actual plan to break into the Democratic National Headquarters in the Watergate Building, he definitely was guilty of trying to cover it up."

I said, "It's hard to understand how a president who was very popular with the American public, having ended an unpopular war and opened relations with China, could be so paranoid about his reelection when he had a comfortable lead in every poll?"

Dennis said, "You hit the nail on the head when you said paranoid. Nixon always felt the Liberal-Democratically controlled newspapers and television networks were out to get him. Remember, this is a man who had lost several elections in his past for which he blamed the press. I think he just let his fear get the best of him. He wouldn't be the first man to do so."

I said, "Maybe that's true, but I think it just shows how corrupt politicians are and our government is. First, Vice President Agnew resigns, and then he's indicted for taking bribes while he was the Governor of Maryland. And now, President Nixon resigns to escape being impeached. I don't think Americans are going to trust politicians for a long time. They're all crooks. What we need to do is clean house."

Dennis said, "Did you know that, originally, members of congress were not paid and nearly all of them served only one or two terms? That's why George Washington served only two terms. He felt a democracy would only work if power was shared, and when someone occupies an elected office for too long, it disrupts the balance of power, and too much power can only lead to corruption."

"Are you saying corruption is inevitable?" I asked

"No," Dennis said, "I'm saying that a man's heart struggles with doing what he knows is right. None of us are perfect. We all fail now and then. Greed, lust, hatred, and retribution, are strong temptations and sometimes people with too much power start to think they're invincible or smarter than everyone else, and start to believe they will never get caught."

So I asked, "What's the solution?"

Dennis replied, "I don't know, I try and not think about politics too much, but I do think term limitations would be a good thing."

I asked Dennis, "Are you a democrat or a republican?"

"I'm an independent," he said.

I said, "Politics are always an interesting topic at our house. Mom's a republican and Dad's a democrat, and when people come to visit, Dad always likes to stir up a debate.

I asked Dad one time how he can be a democrat when everything he believes in is represented by the republican party. He told me, 'The greatest president we've ever had was Franklin Roosevelt, and he was a democrat, and so I will always be one as well.'"

I said, "I think I'm a republican."

Dennis threw several large pieces of wood on the fire and readied himself for bed. He took his shoes off, put his hooded sweatshirt and stocking cap on, folded the rest of his clothes into a pillow, laid down on one half of the tarp, and pulled the other half over himself like a blanket. I followed suit.

The sun came up about 5:00 a.m. The fire had burned down to just glowing embers, so I threw a few sticks on the coals and headed to the restroom. When I got back, Dennis was up and packing his stuff. As I started packing, Dennis left to use the facilities. When he returned, we finished getting ready to leave.

As we continued to pack, Dennis shared with me the secrets of eating while on the road "First, you want to find a restaurant that has on the menu all-you-can-eat pancakes. If you can't, then order extra pancakes. They're usually cheap. Next, ask for peanut butter if they don't have it on the table. Peanut butter makes pancakes taste like candy. Peanut butter is also a great source of protein, and together with the maple syrup, which is nothing but liquid-flavored sugar, you have the perfect energy-packed breakfast. If you drink coffee, you can eat most often for under two bucks, and survive on two meals a day."

"You want to eat a large breakfast when you're hitch-hiking," he said, "Because you can't count on eating lunch. If you don't have a ride, you don't want to leave the road to get lunch because the lunch hour is a peak time for travel, and if you have a ride, it's improper to ask someone to stop so you can eat."

We walked back toward town from the beach and spotted a Pancake House just a few blocks further up Main Street. We sat down and ordered the "special," four large hotcakes and two eggs for $1.99. I put lots of peanut butter on the pancakes, then put the eggs on top, and covered the stack with blueberry syrup. I was definitely full when I had finished.

After using the restroom, which is always a requirement before hitchhiking, we found a telephone booth and called David to get an update on the strike. Having learned no progress had been made, we headed back to Highway 101. As we started to walk, we began another round of the greatest game. The question this time was, Who is America's greatest golfer?

Since I chose the topic, I let Dennis go first, he said, "It would have to be between Jack Nicklaus, Arnold Palmer, or Bobby Jones. I know Nicklaus has won twice as many

Major Championships as Palmer, but Arnold Palmer made golf what it is today. He changed the game from one played only by the rich elite, on exclusive private country clubs, to a game enjoyed by the average, middle-class American. On the other hand, during the era Bobby Jones played in, he had no rivals. He was so much better than his competition, he became a legend. He only played for seven years, but during that time, he won thirteen national championships and the Grand Slam of Golf. More importantly, he played as an amateur never turning professional. So I choose Bobby Jones."

I said, "Well if you're going to choose Bobby Jones, then I have to choose Walter Hagen. Since Hagen defeated Bobby Jones for the World Championship and has more Major Victories than anyone else. Having said that, my favorite is Jack Nicklaus, and I think he will be the greatest golfer of all time if he isn't already."

We were just about to choose which board game is the greatest when we got a ride.

It was just after 7:30 a.m. when a black four-door Chevy Impala with foam dice hanging from the mirror pulled up and offered us a ride. The driver was a high school boy wearing his Letterman's Jacket.

He said, "I'm only going about ten miles, but you're welcome to ride if you want." Remembering Rule Number Four, I said yes.

Seeing he had a football patch on his coat, I asked him what position he played. He said, "Running back, and I also punt."

"How was last year's season?" I said.

"It was okay. We were four and six," he said, "But we will have a senior-dominated team returning, and we're going to win the championship this year." As he pulled over to let us out, I wished him the best of luck.

We hadn't walked more than a couple hundred yards when Dennis stuck out his thumb and a man driving a Dodge pickup pulled over. "Where you headed?" he asked, "I'm headed to Crescent City if you want a ride." We put our things in the back of his pickup and climbed in.

"My name's Terry Vandermeyer," he said, "and I am a hardware salesman. Today, I'm headed south with stops in Bandon, Gold Beach, and Brookings." I've always wondered why people identify themselves by their job, "I'm a teacher," "I'm an accountant," "I'm a business owner." Is that all they really are, or is it just a short answer to a long question?

We introduced ourselves and explained we were headed to San Francisco. Dennis asked Terry how long he'd been a sales representative.

Terry said, "A little over four years. When I got out of the army, I got married, and I needed a job. This one was available. Now I'm divorced, but I have two kids to support, so I'm still working at this job."

I asked him if he liked it. He said, "Yes, I don't mind the travel, but my wife did. I'm never going to get rich, but it pays the bills."

Terry said, "My first stop in Bandon is a short one. If you don't mind waiting about twenty minutes, you're welcome to continue riding along with me."

While Terry met with the manager of the Coast-to-Coast Store, we looked around the store, and then we headed south again. Terry was really no different from the dozen or more people we got rides with that summer, but I think I remember him because of what we talked about during our ride, and what Dennis and I talked about that evening.

As we moved south toward Gold Beach, Dennis shared a little bit of the area's history. "The city is located near where the mouth of the Rogue River enters the Pacific Ocean, and it got its name from the discovery of gold on the beach there in the early 1850s. Hundreds of miners flocked to the beach to pan for gold, and for a short time, it was easy to find. But by the time the vast majority of would be gold miners arrived, the gold rush was over."

"The influx of so many whites into the area brought about conflicts between the local Native Americans and the local settlers and miners. The result was a series of attacks on the Gold Beach settlement, twenty-five to thirty settlers died before soldiers from Fort Humboldt in California could arrive to put down the rebellion. A local legend has it the leader of the Indian uprising captured the regional Indian agent, cut out his heart, and ate it to gain his courage. He and other leaders who led the attacks escaped being captured by the soldiers, but as a result, all the other Native Americans in the area were placed on a reservation."

Terry told us today, Gold Beach is probably most well-known for being the base of the US Mail Boats, one of only two rural mail routes remaining in the United States where the mail is delivered by boat. Terry told us he had several customers to call on in Gold Beach, and it would be several hours before he continued south. So when we reached there, we thanked him for the ride and began hitchhiking again.

– 7 –

OUR NEXT RIDE took us from Gold Beach to Crescent City, California. The man had a hollow smile, and wasn't much for conversation. I'm surprised he stopped to give us a ride; he wasn't overtly friendly. Both Dennis and I tried to get him to talk but neither of us was successful. While Dennis spent most of the time enjoying the view, I tried to figure out more about this person. He had on a black knit shirt with black pants, and there were a pair of black gloves on the seat. Who wears black in the summer time? Maybe he's a bank robber trying to escape the police, and he just picked us up in case he needed hostages. Once, while staying with a friend, I saw a man all dressed in black walking suspiciously around my friend's neighborhood. That night, we learned a house down the street had been broken into. The next day, I saw the same man at the lake. He was wearing black swim-trunks. I ran to tell someone, but when I got back, he had disappeared.

I never saw him again. Since then, I have always been leery of anyone dressed all in black.

Then I thought, *Maybe he's not a bank robber but he's with the FBI, and he's following a bank robber, we have been following the same car for miles.* I finally decided he was a famous actor who didn't want to be recognized. He did look a lot like Paul Newman. Finally, the sound of Dennis's voice awoke me from my daydreaming.

He said, "Our goal for the day is to get to Eureka, California, where we will spend the night on the beach."

Our last ride of the day came courtesy of the Church of God Youth Bus from North Bend, Oregon. The bus, filled with middle school and high school-age students, was headed first to the Redwoods, and then on to Lake Shasta to go water-skiing. Since their evening destination happened to be the same as ours, we accepted the ride. As we entered the bus, I could feel Dennis's apprehension. I wasn't sure if he felt uncomfortable being around so many boisterous teenagers or if he was afraid they were going to witness to him about God. So when several of the students moved forward to talk to us, I tried to defuse the situation. I told them about ourselves and what we were doing. Then I told them about a game we play called The Greatest Game. I asked them, besides Jesus, who's the greatest Bible character. I explained to them you have to name the character, and then explain why you think they are the greatest, you must try to convince everyone else you're right, and no one can have the same character.

The first student to speak was James, a well-built, strong-looking young man. He said, "I choose Noah. If it hadn't been for Noah and his faith, none of us would be alive today. God looked down on the world and saw so much evil. He contemplated destroying all of creation, but God changed his mind because of Noah. God instructed Noah to build an Ark because He was going to flood the earth and destroy all of humankind except for Noah, his family, and a remnant of all the animals. Once it started raining, it rained for forty days and nights. Noah, his family, and the animals were safe, but every other human on the earth died. When the flood subsided, Noah and his family once again repopulated the earth."

The second student to speak was Elizabeth, a young woman who had just graduated from high school like myself, and was headed to Oregon State University in a few weeks; I had to give her a hard time being a Washington State Cougar fan myself.

She said, "I would have to choose Paul as the greatest Bible character other than Jesus. I thought about either Adam or Eve, but I think Paul is the greatest because God chose him to spread the Good News of salvation through Christ Jesus to the Gentiles. Paul was a Jewish zealot who, at first, believed the followers of Christ were infidels, so he persecuted them, believing that's what God would want him to do. Then God struck him down on the road with a bright light, and tells him Jesus is his Son, and the followers of Jesus are not against God but instead believers in God. God then instructs Paul to spread the Good News of Jesus to the non-Jewish world of the Gentiles."

I said, "Wow, both of those are good choices."

The third student to speak was Natalie, a petite young blond. She said, "It has to be Mary, Jesus's mother. God chose her to give birth to his only Son. Mary was engaged to Joseph, but before they were married, an Angel came to Mary and told her she would have a child, and this child would be the Savior of the world. When Mary told Joseph she was pregnant, and what the angel had told her, he didn't believe her, until an angel spoke to him. Without Jesus's birth, Jesus can't die, and if Jesus doesn't die, there is no price paid for our sins, and we can't be redeemed."

The last student to speak was Andrew, a tall and lanky boy with an acne problem. He said, "All of your choices are good, but I think Peter is the best choice. Jesus chose Peter to be the foundation on who God would build the Christian Church. Jesus didn't choose Peter because he was perfect, but just the opposite, because he was imperfect. Peter represents us, even though we believe, and put our trust in God, it doesn't mean we won't have problems in our lives, or we will always succeed in living up to God's perfect standards. After the crucifixion of Jesus, Peter denied ever knowing Jesus three times because he feared being arrested and killed himself. Like Peter, we have to live with our human fears and emotions here on earth, and they sometimes cause us to make mistakes we know are wrong. We won't be perfect until we reach heaven."

I said, "How true, I have often thought in the dictionary under *hypocrite*, they could put the word *Christian* as a synonym because to the outside world, that's what we often look like, someone who says one thing and acts or behaves in a different manner. Isn't it great God looks at our heart and not our actions! But we must always remember we are to be a light to the world, and our behavior can diminish that light."

I asked Dennis, "Who do you think won?"

After a long moment of silence, the bus driver, who had been listening to the whole conversation, said, "I would declare it a tie. You all chose great Bible characters, and made your cases eloquently."

Dennis finally responded. He agreed.

I said, "I know another game if you want to play it."

Natalie said, "I'm game. What is it, and how do you play?"

"It's called mini-mysteries," I said, "I will give you a short clue, and then you have to solve the mystery by asking only questions. I will respond to you with either a yes or no."

Everyone who had played before wanted to play, plus Dennis and the bus driver.

I said, "We will do an easy one, first. Tom and Jerry are dead, how did they die?"

Andrew asked, "Did Tom kill Jerry?"

"No."

Elizabeth said, "Was it an accident?"

"Yes."

The bus driver shouted, "Was a gun used?"

"No."

Andrew said, "Were they killed at the same time, by the same person?"

I said, "That's two questions, and the answers are yes and no."

James said, "Did the bulldog kill them?"

Dennis asked, "Are Tom and Jerry cartoon characters?"

"No."

Natalie said, "No!"

"Are they people?"

"No."

James asked, "Are they animals?"

"No."

"Are they alive," Andrew asked.

"Yes."

The bus driver shouted again, "Do they fly or swim?"

"Yes."

"Are they fish?" Elizabeth asked.

"Yes."

"Did something eat them?" Dennis asked.

"No."

Andrew said, "Did they die of natural causes?"

"No."

"Did they die from lack of oxygen?" asked Natalie.

"Yes."

"So I solved it," Natalie said.

"No."

"What do you mean?" asked Natalie.

"You know what killed them," I said, "But not how they died."

Dennis said, "You said a person didn't kill them, so did something else kill them?"

"Yes."

"Did an animal kill them?" James asked.

"Yes."

"Did a cat kill them?" James asked.

"Yes."

Natalie screamed, "I think I got it, I think I got it! Did the cat drink all the water in their fish bowl?"

"No."

The bus driver said, "Did the cat knock over their fish bowl?"

"Yes."

"Can you solve it," I said.

The bus driver said, "The cat was trying to catch the fish with his paw and accidentally tipped over the fish bowl spilling the water and fish on to the floor, where they died of asphyxiation."

"Yes."

"That was an easy one," James said.

I asked, "Do you want to play another?"

Andrew said, "I'm getting tired. Can you tell us another one, and then give us the answer so we don't have to guess?"

"Sure," I said, "And then you can tell it to someone else."

"A man leaves home, and when he returns home, he finds another man there, with something he doesn't want him to have. What it is it?

"The answer is a baseball."

"Everyone always thinks *home* is the man's house, but *home* is actually home plate. A man leaves home, and when he returns home, he finds another man there, with something he doesn't want him to have."

"That's good, really good, I'm going to try and remember it," Elizabeth said.

A few minutes later, the bus pulled into the parking lot of the Redwood National Park Information Center, and everyone disembarked to see the sites, to smell the fresh air, and experience the beauty of the magnificent ancient Redwood Forest. As we waited for one of the Park Rangers to give us an informative talk, Dennis and I walked around the base of several of the giant redwood trees. I peered into the sky to see where the tops of the trees ended and the sky began.

The park ranger told us the National Park was created in 1968 to complement several smaller state parks. At one time, the giant redwood trees covered over two million acres along the northern coast of California, but by the early 1960s, only 300,000 acres remained; today, between the state parks and the National Park, all of the larger groves are now protected.

After looking through all the exhibits, we boarded the bus and traveled down the road to maybe the most famous of the Redwood Forest attractions, the redwood tree you can drive your car through. You can drive a large car through it, as we witnessed, but buses are not allowed. I picked up several postcards before we boarded the bus again.

We traveled a few more miles to a trailhead where we got off the bus to walk a two-mile nature trail through the forest. The trail wound through the trees, across a creek, up a hill to a viewpoint, and then back down to the starting point. There were so many amazing sights; there were ferns over six feet tall, some had to be nearly eight feet tall. One of the trees near the creek had a watermark on it showing how high the water reached during a flood that happened before recorded history of the area. Which made me think about if these trees could talk, what could they tell us? Some of these trees are two thousand years old. They were already a thousand years old when Columbus discovered America; they were alive before the birth of Christ, one of the high school students pointed out.

After the hike, we rode the bus the last few miles into Eureka, where we thanked them for the ride. They headed to a local church where they were spending the night. We searched for a place to eat and to make a few phone calls. I called home, and my mother answered the phone. I told her we were in Eureka and we were having fun. I didn't talk very long, I've always hated telephones. Dennis called Austin to get an update on the strike. After dinner, we made our way to the beach. Dennis chose a place a little more secluded than last night. We dragged up some firewood, and laid out our provisions, then we stripped down to our swim trunks and sunbathed for a while before taking a swim in the ocean. I had never swum in the ocean before; all I had ever done was wade. The ocean in our region is too cold to swim in, but the ocean's temperature in Northern California was much more amenable. We waited until nearly dusk before starting a fire, just resting and enjoying the sun.

While we were sunbathing, Dennis asked me where I got the mini-mysteries. I said from Mr. Stuart, my high school chemistry teacher. He used to tell us about them to make us think outside the box. He always used to say, "You don't sit on your brains, so learn to use them, exercise them like they're a muscle, and they will grow." I didn't learn a lot about chemistry in his class, but I learned a lot about life from him. He always called me by my father's name. He'd say Glen, and I'd say my name is Nathan, and he'd say I know Glen. He was my father's high school teacher, and he called everyone in class by their parents' name. Chemistry class had thirteen boys in it. Originally, it had seventeen students, but the four girls transferred out a day or two after the class started. He was a great teacher, but everyone thought he was mean. The doors in our high school opened out into the hall rather than into the classroom; if Mr. Stuart heard someone running down the hall, he'd fling open his door. More than once, he knocked out the runner cold. Stories like these were always circulating about him, whether they were true, I don't know, but no one ever ran through his part of the hallway.

One time, a teacher unplugged the jukebox in the student commons because they didn't like the song. The whole school protested; student leaders organized a school wide sit-in. There wasn't a student in any class except for the thirteen boys in Mr. Stuart's chemistry class. Because we knew if we weren't in class, he'd come and find us, pick us up by the back of the neck, and drag us to class. We loved that old man.

As I reviewed the day's travel in my head, I thought about Terry, and how sad he seemed when he talked about his divorce. Without thinking about it, too much, I asked Dennis why he got divorced. At first, I think he was a little shocked by the question, but after a few seconds, he said, "If I had to point to one thing, I guess I don't really know. Instead, I think it was probably a series of poor choices made by both of us. A marriage is hard work, and not something to rush into, which we did. More importantly, there has to be some common ground you can build on. Never confuse infatuation with love. Just because she's pretty is not a good reason. Men are completely visual and too many equate sex appeal with love. Did you know it takes about thirty seconds for a man to fall in love, or what they think is love?

"We didn't do a lot of talking before we got married, which was probably our first mistake, and our common ground was we both liked to party. Building a future on alcohol and drugs is a disaster waiting to happen."

"Do you think you will ever get married again?" I asked.

Dennis smiled like only Dennis could, and said, "You ask too many questions."

I said, "I enjoyed the redwoods today. I knew they were huge, but until I actually saw them, I didn't imagine how big they really are."

Dennis said, "I didn't like riding on the bus, it was too loud, and it reminded me of being on a field trip in middle school. I don't really like kids, especially little ones. My wife wanted to have a baby, and I didn't, that's probably another thing we should have talked about before we got married."

Changing the subject, I asked Dennis if he found there to be anything different since the last time he made this trip.

He said, "It's pretty much the same, the coast doesn't really seem to change that much. I am surprised about the lack of cars on the road; usually this highway is burnt up during the summer time with traffic."

I said, "I'm not surprised, with the price of gas doubling in the last nine or ten months because of the Middle East oil embargo, I'm sure a lot of people are traveling less this summer."

Dennis asked me, "What's your take on the oil embargo and the gas shortage?"

I said, "I think the Arab nations are punishing America for its support for Israel, and they are taking advantage of our dependency on foreign oil. One thing's for sure, if they can hold us hostage once, unless something changes, they will do it again."

Dennis said, "I think it's really a conspiracy between the big oil companies and the Arab nations to force the industrialized world to pay more money for fuel so they can line their pockets with bigger profits. I think they better be careful, governments can and have been overthrown in the past, and countries have nationalized their oil reserves and oil companies. I don't think Americans are going to allow the price of gas to climb to eighty or ninety cents a gallon."

I said, "You may be right!"

Switching subjects again, I said, "As we were walking through the redwoods, I was struck by is how anyone can look at all the wonders of nature and not believe in God. Anyone who believes in evolution must be either very naive or just plain stupid! I have a new theory, and I'm going to call it the theory of de-evolution. My theory is life didn't evolve by chance because of millions of years of random events, but instead, all life forms we know today and probably thousands we will never know about were here once in a perfect form, and since that point have slowly devolved. I think there is more evidence to support my theory than there is to support the theory of evolution."

"Charles Darwin proposed in his essay, *On the Origin of Species* all life evolved through a series of stages. Darwin drew his conclusions from years of observing nature. He concluded since there were differences between species (human, animal, and plant) found in remote locations around the world, each species must have evolved separately.

"He also theorized life forms changed through natural selection, the evolution of mutant attributes made some members of species stronger than others and more fit to survive. Those less fit died off, or their numbers were diminished, as the mutant life forms became the dominant form.

"Darwin's work became the foundation for the theory of evolution; all life forms began as single cells that were somehow created by the combination of random events over millions or billions of years.

"Let me give you a comparative example of this kind of probability," I said, "If I was to take a million-piece jigsaw puzzle, and throw all the pieces into the world's oceans and seas randomly, and give it enough time, all the pieces would find each other, and one day, the completed puzzle would wash ashore.

"If you can't believe this scenario could happen, how can you believe in the theory of evolution, my scenario has a much better chance of happening, than the theory of evolution?

"A better explanation of why there are differences between species in different areas is not species evolved separately; but all forms of the same species once existed at the same time, but some species no longer exist in all areas of the world due to environmental conditions or human intervention.

"The idea of mutant attributes being a positive thing, can't be substantiated by any physical evidence. What can be substantiated is the corruption of a life form's DNA, has a negative impact, and most mutations die immediately or have very short life spans, which doesn't support the theories of survival of the fittest or natural selection.

"Have you ever heard of the Golden Ratio or the Fibonacci Code? Leonard Fibonacci was a scientist and mathematician, and while researching the reproduction rates of rabbits, he discovered a natural law of physics; later, scientists would call it the Golden Ratio, or sometimes the Divine Ratio. A simple explanation of the Golden Ratio is most living things grow proportional, an example is a tree. There is mathematical relationship between the number of limbs a tree has, and the distance between the limbs, which can be defined as a mathematic ratio. This ratio is what gives the tree its symmetry. This same ratio can be found in nearly all life forms, it's found repeatedly in the human body. One example is our fingers—each finger consists of four bones. In terms of length, the smallest bone is at the tip of your finger, if you add its length to the length of the second bone, their length equals the length of the third bone, and if you add the length of the second bone and the third bone, together it equals the length of the fourth and final bone. Once again, this ratio gives our human bodies its symmetry or proportional beauty.

"The theory of evolution is based upon chaos, upon constant change, a continuous selection process; the Fibonacci Code and the Golden Ratio show us how life is not a random process but instead a divine creation. God is a mathematician!"

Dennis said, "For argument's sake, let me play the devil's advocate, and ask you some questions. According to your theory, all species alive today or lived in the past, occupied the earth together?"

"My theory does not preclude that," I said.

"So how do you explain the dinosaurs," Dennis said, "How could man have competed against them, and why didn't whatever wiped them out, wipe out the human race as well?"

"There are several possible explanations for the dinosaurs," I said. "If you accept the Bible's version of creation as told in Genesis chapter one, God created all things in a series of days. On the sixth day, God created both the animals who roam the earth, but also man and woman. So it's clear both the dinosaurs and humans existed at the same time, but while they co-existed together, doesn't mean they interacted with each other. God placed man in the Garden, a specified area of the earth clearly to be the realm of man, and not the realm of animals including dinosaurs. While the Bible describes the fall of man, when Adam and Eve sinned, it does not tell us how many years they lived in the Garden before they were banished. They could have been there millions of years. The dinosaurs may have already met their demise prior to Adam and Eve's fall from grace, or

God's protection of them in the Garden kept them safe from the same outside forces that killed the dinosaurs.

"A second explanation could be when God created the animals, he didn't distribute them equally across the earth. It could have taken many millennia for them to spread out across the world, and they would have had to traverse many barriers such as mountains, rivers, deserts, etc. as part of their migration.

"Another possibility is as the earth separated itself into different continents from one large land mass called Pangaea, the dinosaurs, and other animal populations were greatly diluted in numbers, making coexistence with them much more possible. There may or may not have been much, if any contact between the two. I'd also say dinosaurs are a prime example of de-evolution. Once they were here, but due to changing weather conditions, being hunted by man, or disease, they now are extinct. They disappeared; they didn't evolve into another species."

Dennis said, "Give me another example that supports your theory."

"Okay, humans," I said. "We have recorded histories showing man at one time lived to be six, seven, even eight hundred years old before they died. Today, the average man barely lives long enough to collect his social security. Due to the corruption of the genes we pass on to our posterity over time, we live shorter lives today. We have more retardation, more people born with abnormalities, more people born with hereditary diseases."

"Wow, you've thought about this a lot," Dennis said. "How about we talk about something a little less heavy before we go to sleep, like what's the greatest board game of all time?"

"Okay," I said. "Who gets to go first?"

"Let's flip a coin," Dennis said., "I win"

"I choose Monopoly. It's the greatest selling board game of all time, and nearly three-quarters of all American households have a copy of the game in their home. It involves skill, chance, risk, and strategy."

"Good choice," I said. "But not as good as mine. I thought you were going to choose chess or checkers. If we were talking about the greatest American game it would have to be checkers, but my choice for the greatest board game of all time is chess. It is the ultimate board game of strategy."

Dennis smiled and said, "I plead no contest this time."

I asked him if he had ever played Manacula.

He said, "No, I've never heard of it."

I said, "It's an African game. I played it at a friend's house a while back. It's fun and it's been played for over four thousand years."

Dennis said, "That's cool, do you know where chess was created?"

"I'd have to say England, because of the playing pieces king, queen, knight, and castle."

"Good guess," he said. "But it was originally created in India and the playing pieces were changed during the middle ages to appease western European nobility."

Having spent so much time talking about games, we decided to play a few hands of rummy and then a game of spades before we called it a night.

– 8 –

WHEN WE AWOKE the next morning, the temperature had already reached the mid-sixties. Dennis said, "Let's go for a swim in the ocean. This will be our last chance. Today, we should reach San Francisco." So we swam for a while then cleaned up in a fresh-water pond, packed up our supplies and headed into town for breakfast, two eggs, and hotcakes with peanut butter. Before we left the restaurant, Dennis called Austin to check in, and with no progress to report, we once again began hitchhiking.

We had barely left the restaurant when we got our first and only ride of the day. In fact, we were still in the restaurant parking lot. It came courtesy of two young women (see rule number five) who were on vacation themselves. We were both leaving the restaurant at the same time; they saw we had our backpacks on and were walking and asked us where we were headed. Their names were Shelia and Rosemary, and they were driving Shelia's 1972 red convertible Ford Mustang. They were from Southern California, and as it turned out, their destination for the day was the same as ours, San Francisco. They had spent time in San Francisco on their way north so they planned to just spend the night there as they were headed back home. Shelia was a nurse and Rosemary worked as court stenographer. They both appeared to be in their mid-twenties. Shelia was the taller of the two, and slimmer as well, not that either of them were overweight. She was wearing a shoulder-less top and her shoulders were pink from sunburn, they had obviously driven much of the trip with the top down on the convertible Mustang. Rosemary, while being shorter, was well-proportioned, with black hair that flowed down her back to nearly her waist. With the top down, her hair blew in the wind like a windsock.

After we had traveled a few miles, I asked them what they liked most about their vacation so far.

Shelia said, "I liked Big Sur, the scenery along the coast is breathtaking, we stopped and took the tour of Hearst Castle. It was interesting."

"What was interesting?" Dennis asked.

"I especially liked the tapestries that hang from the walls like murals, the painted ceilings, and the swimming pools," she said.

"I liked Cannery Row in Monterey the best," Rosemary said. "It has lots of great places to shop, some of the shops are located in the original cannery factories. You can still see the old conveyor belts overhead."

Rosemary said, "I think we both enjoyed the Napa Valley. It's very quaint, and we are planning to stop there again for lunch."

"Did you know there's a geyser in Calistoga known as the Old Faithful Geyser of California?" Shelia asked. "I didn't know it until we went there. It spouts about every forty minutes, and its spray reaches about sixty feet high and last for around three minutes. It's just as cool as Old Faithful in Yellowstone."

When Rosemary finished, Shelia said, "I enjoyed the redwoods and Fisherman's Wharf in San Francisco as well. The Wharf is a great place to eat and shop, we spent all day there. We took the cable car ride up Nob Hill where you get a great view of the city, but the thing we had the most fun doing in San Francisco was visiting Alcatraz Island."

Seeing neither one was wearing a wedding ring, Dennis asked them how two such beautiful women were not married? They both laughed, and asked the same of him, clearly they viewed me as too young for anything other than conversation.

I asked if they had ever heard of the greatest game, and explained it was something we play to pass the time. They said no, but they were willing to play. Remembering Rule

Number Three, keep the conversation about them, I said, "Great, does anybody have a topic?"

Shelia said, "The greatest American woman."

Rosemary said, "Who goes first?"

Dennis said, "Whose birthday comes first."

Rosemary said, "Mine is March 15, 1952."

Dennis said, "The Ides of March, the day Julius Caesar was assassinated."

"Shelia's is June 22, 1952," she continued. "We graduated from Jefferson High School in 1969 and have been roommates for the past two years."

I said, "I'm definitely last. My birthday is in August, 1956."

Dennis said, "I guess I'm first since I was born in December, 1946."

"I would have to choose Abigail Adams," Dennis said, "The wife of President John Adams. You know the saying behind every good man is a good woman; well, Abigail Adams is the epitome of this saying, except in this case, it should be said behind every good man is a great woman. Abigail was well-educated and the closest confidant of John. John spent significant amounts of time away from home, and he often felt he was a man on a mission without support from anyone other than his wife. Abigail and John corresponded extensively by letters, through which John shared his thoughts about declaring independence from

England, and the formation of a new government. She was his sounding board; she openly expressed her opinions about his ideas, and freely gave John her own. John Adams is the most instrumental historical figure in the formation of this country, and Abigail deserves much of this credit as well. When John Adams became president, Abigail sets the standard for all first ladies to follow. She is also the mother of President John Quincy Adams."

Rosemary said, "I'm next, and I choose another president's wife, Eleanor Roosevelt. She was not the woman behind the man; he was the man in front of the woman. No one has ever been a more shrewd, aggressive, and powerful political organizer. Franklin D. Roosevelt, known by most as FDR, had been groomed since birth to be President of the United States by his mother. She even chose Eleanor to be his wife, but when FDR was struck with polio at age forty, his mother gave up on the dream. But Eleanor didn't give up. After a period of recovery and rehabilitation, she revived his political career by working tirelessly behind the scenes. Once he was elected president, it's said nothing happened in the White House or in the FDR administration without her approval. Shelia, it's your turn!"

"I choose Elizabeth Cady Stanton," she said. She's the most notable founder of the Women's Rights Movement in America. In the mid-eighteen century, Stanton and others formed the first formal Women's Rights Organization.

These leaders and those who followed are responsible for our right to vote and all other equalities women have gained. It's said that when Elizabeth got married, she refused to go through with it, unless the word obey was omitted from the ceremony. Once women were the property of their father, or their husband, and had no legal status or the right to own property. Now we can work, own property, and be whatever we want to be, thanks to Elizabeth Cady Stanton."

"Since I'm last, I get the choice of everyone else," I said. "I thought I'd throw a few names out and see if I got any reactions before choosing one. I've been thinking about Amelia Earhart, Jacqueline Kennedy, Marilynn Monroe, and Narcissa Whitman," I said. I saw a little spark in Rosemary's eye when I mentioned Jacqueline Kennedy, so that's who I decided on. "Jacqueline Kennedy is the most influential woman of the twentieth century. She's the closest thing to American royalty we've had since George Washington. Jacqueline was the calm in a chaotic world, the media loved her, women adored her, and she had more style and grace than any previous first lady. She not only stole the spotlight from the president when they traveled abroad, but she became an icon for every American woman. When JFK died, all of America felt her pain, and admired her fortitude. She will forever be remembered for her inner strength during a personal and national tragedy."

Rosemary said, "How do we decide who wins?"

"We see if there is a consensus," Dennis said.

"I would vote for Shelia and Stanton," he said.

I said, "I had a hunch you might."

Rosemary said, "I agree as well, every living American woman owes a debt of gratitude to Elizabeth Cady Stanton, including Eleanor Roosevelt and Jacqueline Kennedy."

Shelia said, "What would make you think Marilynn Monroe deserves such credit?" I said, "The greatest pinup girl of all time has to at least deserve an honorable mention."

"Congratulations, Shelia, you're the winner," Dennis said.

As we neared the Napa Valley, Shelia asked if we'd like to join them for lunch, her treat. Dennis quickly said, "Yes, but only if they'd join us for dinner as our guests." Thirty minutes or so later, we stopped at a winery with a rustic-looking building that doubled as a restaurant and a wine-tasting room. I ordered some kind of mushroom soup with a Pepsi to drink; the others ordered a variety of items and drank wine. Rosemary had already had two glasses of wine, and apparently was about to order a third when Shelia said we needed to be on our way. It didn't seem like it took very long before we reached the Golden Gate Bridge. We stopped at Marin's Vista Point, to take in the San Francisco cityscape, before heading down to the waterfront to find a hotel near Pier 39.

As we checked in, Dennis asked Shelia and Rosemary if they had visited the Golden Gate Park when they were here earlier. They said no.

"Good," Dennis said. "Get settled in and we'll meet you in the lobby in thirty minutes."

We both took quick showers and cleaned up before heading back to the lobby. From the hotel, we took a series of trolley cars on our way to the park. Dennis told us the park is adjacent to the Haight-Ashbury District made famous by the late 1960s Summer of Love. He said the first time he came to San Francisco, there were people everywhere, music on every street corner, people protesting, others preaching the power of peace, love, and Proud Mary. Young people from every part of the country were here. He said, "The Golden Gate Park was one of the places he and hundreds of others camped during their stay. It's a beautiful place with several different gardens."

The first place we visited was the Conservatory of Flowers, a glass structure modeled after a famous glass house in London. It's renowned for its beautiful orchids. Next, we visited the Japanese Tea Garden filled with cherry trees, bonsai trees, and bridges that crossed tranquil ponds filled with koi. We finished our visit by walking around Stow Lake, famous for the artificial island in the center of the lake known as Strawberry Hill. By the end of Dennis's tour, it was near dusk, so we boarded a trolley and headed back toward our hotel and Fisherman's Wharf, where we ate dinner. Once again, Rosemary drank too much. When we finished dinner, Dennis and Shelia headed for Chinatown, while Rosemary and I headed back to the hotel.

It didn't seem right to leave Rosemary by herself so I invited her to come up to our room to watch TV. She sat down on the couch, and I turned on the TV to the Late Night News. Rosemary was clearly intoxicated and started crying, and then she started telling me why they were on vacation.

She said, "About a year ago, I met this new law clerk who worked for one of the judges I'm a stenographer for, he was clerking while he studied to take the bar exam. He was from back east, just out of law school, and didn't know anyone in Los Angeles, so we struck up a friendship. After a few weeks, he asked me out, one thing led to another, and we became romantically involved. I helped him study a couple nights a week and he took me out to fancy restaurants and nightclubs. We even talked about moving in together, and I told him I loved him, that's when he told me he was engaged. He got married a week ago, and now he's on his honeymoon, while I'm taking a trip up the California Coast, getting drunk every night, and crying myself to sleep. That's why Shelia went with Dennis, she's tired of listening to me cry every night."

I gave her some tissues, and tried to tell her everything always turns out for the best, but I had no clue what to say or do next. Thankfully, the alcohol kicked in, and she passed out on the couch. I watched the rest of the news and the Johnny Carson show then fell asleep myself. About 2:00 a.m., Dennis and Shelia came in, and we helped Rosemary back to her room. I felt sorry for Rosemary, so I prayed for her before I drifted off to sleep again, which must have happened quickly because I don't remember Dennis coming back in. When I awoke the next morning, he was taking a shower, and telling me to hurry up, we had a lot to do today. I asked if we were having breakfast with the girls. He said no, they've already left. I said, "Too bad, I would have liked to have said good-bye."

Dennis said, "You can send them a postcard. I've got their phone number and address." We ate breakfast, and then hurried to catch the next ferry to Alcatraz Island.

Dennis said, "I've been to San Francisco several times, but I've never been to the island."

When we left the hotel, it appeared as if the whole world was blanketed in fog. I could barely see more than fifty feet in front of myself. Once we were on the ferry, the tour guide explained during the summer, San Francisco often gets heavy fog. Sometimes, the city is socked in all day, but most often, it burns off by early afternoon. It was so eerie crossing to the island; shrouded in mist, the sounds of the bay were magnified. You could hear the foghorns and bells from other ships, I was terrified we were going to run into another ship, or worse, one would run into us. But we made it, and we saw Al Capone and Machine Gun Kelly's prison cells, and where the Bird Man raised his pigeons. It was cold and damp there, but by the time we boarded the ferry for the return trip, the fog had lifted, and it felt more like summer and less like a cold winter day in the northwest.

After docking back in San Francisco, we took the trolley cars once again back to the Haight-Ashbury district to walk around. The blocks are filled with small shops, eateries, and pubs. Dennis showed me the place where the Grateful Dead once lived, and Janis Joplin's house. I knew "Me and Bobby McGhee," but I couldn't tell him the name of one single Grateful Dead song. As we ate lunch at a small street side eatery, we spent time people watching. You could see dozens of others who'd come to the HA on this day to either reminisce about past years, or to visit the place where terms such as *Flower Power* and *Peace Out* were coined. As we walked the streets, I could see the gleam in Dennis's eyes as he told me stories. I was happy we had made this trip if for no other reason than to experience San Francisco through his eyes.

It was early evening by the time we returned to the hotel. I called my parents to check in and let them know

I was still alive. I told them I was sending them several postcards of some of the places we had visited, and I loved them. Along with the postcards I sent my parents, I sent one to Rosemary. I told her not waste her tears on thoughts about the past, instead move forward and love will find her. I wrote, "The creator of love is God, so you might want to start your journey by attending a church. My father has always said you can never go wrong with a Baptist church." Dennis called and checked in with Austin, there was no progress to report on the strike. He sent a postcard as well, but he didn't say to whom.

We walked to Chinatown to have dinner, it was the best Chinese food I had ever eaten, and there was so much, we took back plenty for later to snack on. As we ate, I asked Dennis where we were headed next, he pulled out his pocket road atlas, and said, "I think we'll head toward Reno, then on to Denver. I've got a good buddy from the army who lives in a town just outside of Denver called Loveland."

I said, "Groovy."

Dennis said, "It's set then. Tomorrow morning we'll make our way to Highway 80 and stick out our thumbs towards Reno, Nevada. But tonight we have plenty of leftover Chinese food and a soft bed to sleep in."

As we finished eating, we read our Chinese fortune cookies. Mine said, "History is more than the past. It's a window to the future."

"You are about to be reunited with a friend from the past," Dennis read.

I said, "How weird is that!"

Dennis said, "I bet you don't know where the Chinese fortune cookie originated."

I said, "China?"

He said, "No, San Francisco. A Japanese immigrant created the cookies around 1915. He was a landscaper and the manager of the Japanese Tea Garden in Golden Gate Park, where he served the cookies with tea. The story is the owner of a nearby Chinese restaurant saw their popularity and added fortune cookies to his menu as dessert."

I said, "How did you know that?"

"I've been to San Francisco several times, and I read it on the back of a Chinese restaurant's menu."

— 9 —

I N THE MORNING, we ate the rest of the Chinese food from the night before instead of having breakfast. We checked out of the hotel, and made our way to the closest I-80 on ramp. As the city woke up, it found itself covered in a blanket of fog again, which didn't help us as we were trying to hitch a ride. With such low visibility, we stood at the base of the entrance ramp for probably twenty minutes before we got a ride, but it was a good one. Our ride was a small, white delivery truck; the painted sign on the side of the truck said Santino's Fresh Seafood Company. When the truck pulled over, the driver rolled the window down and asked about our destination. We said Reno; he said, "I can give you a ride as far as Sacramento if you want."

I opened the door and climbed in first, scooting into the center between Dennis and our host. Glad it was a truck with a shift on the column and not a stick-shift on the floor. Our host introduced himself a Joe Santino.

I said, "I'm Nathan and this is Dennis." As Joe sped up the entrance ramp and on to the freeway, he said, "I like picking up hitchhikers, it gives me someone to talk to." I asked Joe if he owned Santino's Fresh Seafood Company.

He said, "Yes, me and my wife are the owners. We bought it from my uncle about five years ago. We buy the best seafood we can each morning from the fishermen, and deliver it fresh to our customers. Mostly, we sell shrimp, crab, salmon, tuna, and halibut. Most of our customers are restaurants and small grocery stores. Today's route takes me to Sacramento and Stockton."

Dennis asked Joe how long he'd been selling fresh seafood. He said, "I worked for my uncle for about ten years before we bought the business, so I've been doing this close to sixteen years. What about you guys?"

I said, "I just graduated from high school, and I'm headed off to college this fall."

Dennis said, "I work for a company that builds yachts, but I used to be a chef, and I love cooking with fresh seafood."

Joe said his great grandfather and his two great uncles immigrated to America during the late 1800s along with thousands of other Italian immigrants and settled in the North Beach area of San Francisco. They called it Little Italy. His family has always fished or worked in the seafood industry. "It's in our blood, and someday, I hope to pass this business down to my son."

I said, "My father owns a rock and concrete business, but he wants me to go to college. He's never talked about wanting me to own or run his company someday. He's never even taught me how to run any of the equipment. I think he's afraid I will hurt myself so he lets me do things with him, but never by myself."

Joe said, "So you're headed to Reno to gamble and win big bucks."

"No, were actually headed to a town near Denver, and Reno's just on our way," Dennis said.

Joe said, "So you're not going to gamble."

"I didn't say that. Maybe a little," Dennis said.

"My wife likes to gamble, me not so much. But I take her to Reno a couple of times a year. She actually won a big jackpot five years ago and we used it as the down payment to buy the business from my uncle."

Joe dropped us off at his first stop in Sacramento. We thanked him for the ride and then made our way to Broadway Street which parallels I-80, bought a bottle of pop, and continued hitchhiking.

It was not yet 10:00 a.m., but the temperature had reached the point where you could cook an egg on the sidewalk; even standing on the asphalt next to the freeway, I could feel the soles of my shoes melting. I prayed, *Please, Lord, let our next ride have air-conditioning*, and I was so thankful when it did. They were a young couple driving a crimson-colored Monte Carlo with a white, leather roof with air-conditioning. They were returning from the coast to their home in Twin Falls, Idaho. Luckily for us, their route home took them right through Reno.

Their names were Tim and Diana. They said they didn't usually stop for hitchhikers, but we looked clean cut, and we weren't long hairs, but mostly, I think they felt sorry for us standing in the hot sun. I said, "Thanks for stopping, you're a Godsend." By the time we were finished with our brief introductions and short background stories, the air-conditioning had satisfactorily cooled us down. Tim sold farm equipment and Diana was a stay-at-home mom. They had two children, both boys, three and four years old. They had lived in Twin Falls for the past six years; before that, they had lived in Boise. It's amazing how much people will share about their lives if you just ask a few questions and they feel comfortable, even with total strangers.

They will tell you about the things they're most proud of, their hobbies, and their future plans if you just let them talk. After traveling with them for an hour, I knew Diana was a gardener, and very proud of her flowers. She loves to have fresh-cut flowers in the house for as long as she can each year, so she grows a variety of flowers that bloom throughout the spring and summer. Tim has two hobbies: one is fixing up old cars, and the other is fishing. He loves to fish the Snake River, which runs right through the city of Twin Falls, albeit in a cannon which is several hundred feet deep. Lastly, their future goals are to have two more kids, hopefully a couple of girls, and move back to Boise to be nearer to family. The more I listened, the more I realized how much they seemed to be happy. Unlike some of the others we had met on this trip. I thought to myself, *I hope my life turns out more like theirs and Joe Santino's, and less like Rosemary's and Terry's.*

As we neared the crest of the Sierra Nevada Mountains, Tim and Dennis began talking about cars. Tim said, "If you like cars, you have to visit the Antique Car Museum in Reno."

Dennis said, "That's one of the things I had on my list to do."

Tim was nice enough to drop us off downtown near the famous sign, "Reno the Biggest Little City in the World." We thanked them, as always, and waved as they drove off.

The good things about Reno are one, it's cheap. We got a room for eight bucks in a motel just a few blocks off the main Casino Strip, and two, you can eat great food for a couple of bucks a meal. The Reno City sign says, "It's little and it's true, you can walk just about to everywhere you want to go." After checking into our motel, Dennis called to get an update on the strike.

Austin said, "The two sides have agreed to start talks again, but there is no news to report at this time." So we made plans to continue forward with our travels.

Dennis said, "I want to get to Denver as soon as possible, and I really don't want to hitchhike across the desert."

So we walked to the local Greyhound station to see what it would cost to take the bus. We found out there were buses leaving tomorrow at 7:00 a.m. and 1:00 p.m., and the cost would be twenty-one dollars a ticket. We also learned the eight-hundred-mile trip had three scheduled stops, and would take approximately twelve hours. We bought tickets for the 7:00 a.m. bus.

From the bus depot, we walked to the Antique Car Museum. In my mind, I thought it would be a few old cars someone had collected, but it was much more, it was like an art museum, except the paintings and sculptures were motorized works of art. It was a history lesson of the world's carmakers. There were Model T and Model A Fords, Indianapolis 500 Race Winners from every decade, a Dodge De Soto, a Tucker, and an Edsel. There were also early models of Chryslers, Chevrolets, and vehicles from carmakers I had never heard of. There were foreign cars from Italy, Germany, and British Motor Works models. I learned that Mercedes and Benz were separate cars manufacturers before they teamed up to make today's Mercedes-Benz cars. We were there for two hours, and we could have spent another hour or more, but after two hours, we were tired, so we decided to head back to our motel room to take a nap.

When we awoke from our siesta, it was time for dinner, so we walked back uptown to find a good place to eat. We walked through several of the casinos, checking out their menu prices before we settled on one that had all you can eat for three dollars. After dinner, Dennis said, "Let's play the slot machines." I was apprehensive; every slot machine had a sign on it, "No one under 21. Violators will be prosecuted." I didn't have a lot of money to lose, but I bought two-nickel rolls from the coin girl, and chose a five-cent slot machine to play. It didn't take very long for me to lose my money, so I searched around to find Dennis. I don't know what he started with, but when I found him, he had a bucketful of quarters. After watching him play for a few minutes, I decided to buy one more roll of nickels. I looked around for the girl from whom I had purchased nickels from the first time, but I couldn't find her.

So I approached another coin girl, I said I'd like a roll of nickels, and gave her my money. She eyed me up and down, and I felt like she knew I was underage, but she finally handed me a roll of nickels, and as calmly as possible, I walked away to play again. I decided to try a different slot machine, so I walked around looking for an interesting one before sitting down to play. I was about halfway through my nickels when I hit a jackpot that paid off more money than I had lost, a few more pulls on the same one-armed bandit, and I hit an even bigger jackpot.

I decided the odds the same machine would pay off again were low, so I moved to another slot machine. I found a new machine like the one I had just left, sat down on the stool and began playing again. I continued to win a little here and there, when, suddenly, I felt a tap on my shoulder. I must have jumped two feet high, so much, it startled the server who had tapped me. She smiled and asked if I'd like a drink, I said, no, thank you, and as soon as she left, I gathered up my cash and nearly ran out of the casino. Once out on the street, I took a few deep breaths and let my heart, settle down before I reentered to find Dennis. When I found him I told him what had happened, he laughed so hard, he began choking. I asked Dennis to turn in my change for bills and we left. We walked up and down the core area of downtown Reno, enjoying the lights and the sounds for a few minutes before we called it a night, and headed back to our motel for the evening.

Dennis said we had one more stop before we returned to the motel: a convenience store to purchase a pair of earplugs for tonight and for the bus ride tomorrow. He said, "People will be coming and going from the motel all hours of the night. They walk down the halls, they open and shut doors, and you will never get any sleep tonight without earplugs." So I bought a pair as well, and I never heard a sound.

I awoke at 5:00 a.m., got up, and headed off to take a shower. When I finished, I turned on the morning TV news to watch while Dennis showered. When Dennis finished, we packed up our belongings, and headed toward the Greyhound Station. We stopped by a café on the way and had the advertised special for breakfast, steak and eggs, for two dollars. We saw the same special advertised all over town. I'm not sure why, the combination didn't really work for me. When we got to the bus station, the bus had already arrived, so we bought a couple Payday candy bars, stored our gear, and boarded the bus. There were only a couple other people on the bus, and plenty of room to sit wherever we wanted. Dennis walked to the back of the bus, then forward about ten rows, he said, "Feel the air, this is the strongest place I've felt it, this is where we want to sit." Dennis took the window seat, quickly put his earplugs in, and closed his eyes. I sat in the aisle seat, and watched as the other passengers boarded. There were a couple of families, but mostly, the passengers were single people traveling alone. A woman made her way up the aisle and sat in the seat across from me. Later, another woman asked if she was saving the window seat, and then sat down in the open seat. As the departure time neared, the bus began filling up quickly. Just before we left, four young men boarded and chose to sit in seats near us. As the bus began to roll, I kicked my seat back a little and closed my eyes as well.

I woke a few hours later with an elbow in my ribs from Dennis. I was snoring again. When I finally regained my senses, I introduced myself to those seated around me and apologized for my snoring. As I shook the cobwebs from my head, I sat, silently listening to those around me. The women across from me were talking about their families, the two young men in front of us were boasting about their exploits of the last twenty-four hours to the two young men in the seats across from them. The woman closest to me was on her way to her sister's home in Denver; her youngest sister had just had a baby. The other woman was headed back home to Albuquerque, New Mexico. The four young men in front of us obviously knew each other, and they were all tall, with muscular builds, with the same haircuts. I asked them where they were headed, the young man seated diagonally from me in the aisle seat said they were headed back to the Air Force Academy in Colorado Springs. The four of them where on a forty-eight-hour pass. They had decided to go to Reno stay up all night and return the next morning. I asked the two women and the four young men if they would like to play a game to pass the time. One of the young men asked, "What's the game?"

"It's called The Greatest Game," and I explained how to play. After all six of them had agreed to play, I announced the topic, the greatest TV show.

I told them with eight people playing, this would be interesting. We'll let the women go first, and then the cadets, then Dennis, and I will go last. The woman in the window seat deferred to the other woman.

The woman in the aisle seat said, "My name's Cathy, and the greatest TV show of all time is *Father Knows Best*. The show actually started in the late 1940s as a radio show, and then became a TV show on CBS in the mid-1950s. It stared Robert Young as Jim Anderson, and Jane Wyatt as Mrs. Anderson. The show was about a middle-class family living in the Midwest. I remember watching it as a young girl, and each episode had a moral lesson. It was produced in the same style as *Ozzie and Harriet*, and taught values unlike much of the trash on TV today."

The woman near the window said, "I always liked *The Adventures of Ozzie and Harriet*, I especially liked Ricky Nelson. I had a picture of him on my wall when I was growing up. He was my teenage idol; I must have played his records "Poor Little Fool," "Hello, Mary Lou," and "Travelin Man" a million times. I'm Maria, and I'd say the best TV show of all time would have to be *Gun Smoke*. I think it was a radio show first as well. I remember watching it first on a small black-and-white set, not these humongous color TV consoles they have today. It's the classic Western TV show, with Marshal Dillon, Miss Kitty, Doc

Adams, and Chester. Its set in Dodge City, Kansas, in the 1870s during the era of cattle drives and rustlers. Marshal Dillon is the hero, and he's in love with Miss Kitty, but he never tells her so. I believe it's the longest running program still on TV. I think I heard over six hundred shows of *Gun Smoke* have aired."

I said, "I've only watched *Gun Smoke* a couple of times. Where I live, we only get ABC and NBC. CBS has so many ghosts, we can't watch it. I do like Rickey Nelson, especially his recent hit, "Garden Party."

"Since we are going clockwise, why don't we just continue that direction," I said.

"I guess that means I'm next," Thomas said, "I'm from West Virginia, coal mining country, and I never saw a TV until I was fourteen. We were so poor. Each year, we owed the company store more than we did the year before. One summer, my parents sent me to stay with my cousins in Tennessee, and that's the first time I saw a TV. We did have a movie house in our town, but my brother and I rarely could afford to go watch a matinee, so I'm probably the least qualified to be a judge here. But if I had to pick, I'd chose *Hawaii Five-O*. It's my favorite TV show today; I like the scenery, I'm hoping someday I might be stationed there. I like the theme song, and my favorite character is Danny, I always like it when McGarrett says, "Book 'em, Danno.""

The young man in the aisle seat said, "That's why you're always humming that stupid song."

Afterward, he said, "My name is Josh, and the greatest TV show of all time is *The Twilight Zone*. The show ended in 1964, but you can watch the reruns on Saturday afternoons. It was futuristic and often about the paranormal or unsolved events. Its plot was always full of twist and turns, and you never really understood everything, until the very end of the show. The show always began with the suspenseful voice of the narrator. Glued to the TV, my friends and I would watch, totally engrossed, until the narrator's voice returned to end the show."

The cadet directly in front of me went next. "I'm Danny," he said, "The greatest TV show of all time is *Gilligan's Island*. The premise of the show doesn't make any sense. It's so wacky it's cool. Why would one of the world's richest millionaires and a movie star be on a sightseeing trip with the other characters on this show? The millionaire would have his own yacht, and the movie star wouldn't take all her clothes and furs with her on a one-day trip. The whole scenario is so ridiculous, it has to be the greatest because millions of people tune in to watch it each week. It has no redeeming value other than pure comedy, and after all, isn't that why we watch TV, to be entertained?"

The last cadet introduced himself as Jackson. He said, "I'm torn between *The Avengers* and *Alfred Hitchcock*

Presents, they're both so good. I guess I'd choose *Alfred Hitchcock Presents.* Hitchcock in his slow, droll voice would welcome you to the show. Every episode was a suspense thriller, the best roller coaster ride on TV."

After Dennis introduced himself to the others, he said, "All of your choices are good, but there not as good as the *Rifle Man,* the story of a man and his son trying to survive in the lawless, untamed Wild West. The *Rifle Man* is a modern-day Robin Hood. The son idolizes his father, but is always terrified someone will come along who is faster with a gun than his father is. Most other Western shows have gunfighters who use pistols, not a rifle, which makes it unique."

"I can't believe all of you forgot about *American Bandstand,*" I said. "I thought at least someone would choose it, so I had *Leave it to Beaver* as my backup choice. But Dick Clark's *American Bandstand,* is the greatest TV show of all time. No plot, just dancing and music. It's the show that launched a thousand hits, changed how we dance, and helped shape the 1960s. My sisters watched it every Saturday afternoon; they'd jump around and pretend they were dancing. I'd pretend I had a microphone in my hand, and I would sing all the hits. Back then, I always wanted to be Paul McCartney."

"All right," I said, "let's see who the winner is, and let's make it so you can't vote for yourself."

"Cathy, what's your choice?"

"I vote for *Gun Smoke*," she said.

"What about you, Maria?" I asked.

"I vote for *Alfred Hitchcock*."

"Thomas, what's your vote?"

"I chose Hitchcock as well."

"You're next, Josh," I said.

"I vote for *Gun Smoke*."

"Okay, we have a tie. Two votes for *Gun Smoke*, and two votes for *Alfred Hitchcock Presents*."

"Danny, what's your choice?"

"I really liked your choice of *American Bandstand*, but I don't see it in the same category as the other shows, so I choose *Gun Smoke*. The longest-running show in TV history has to be the greatest TV show of all time, statistics don't lie."

"I disagree," Jackson, said, "It's all in how you define greatest. It could be measured by longevity, but it could also be measured by creativity, and I think Alfred Hitchcock was a master of creativity, so I choose Hitchcock."

"What do you think, Dennis," I said.

"I agree, creativity is the most important factor, but I think the most creative show is not *Alfred Hitchcock Presents* but instead is *The Twilight Zone*."

"Then it's still a tie between *Hitchcock* and *Gun Smoke*," Maria said, "Are you going to break the tie, Nathan?"

"I'm highly disappointed no one voted for *American Bandstand*," I said. They all laughed. "But you don't stay on TV for nineteen years unless you're exceptional, so I choose *Gun Smoke*." Cathy, Josh, and Danny cheered.

— 10 —

Jackson said, "That was fun, let's play again!"

I said, "Okay, does everyone want to play?"

Cathy and Maria said they'd sit this one out, but all the cadets said they were in.

I asked Jackson if he had a topic.

He said, "Yes, who's the greatest professional basketball player of all time."

"Shall I go first this time?" I asked.

Jackson said, "Sure, go ahead."

"Well, I think the greatest professional basketball player of all time is Oscar Robertson. Known as the Big O, he is unquestionably the best all-around player of all time. He's one of the all-time scoring leaders, and one of the best defensive players year in and year out, and he's always at the top of the list in assists and rebounds each year for guards. More importantly, he's a team leader, the glue that makes the Milwaukie Bucks perennial contenders for the NBA

Championship. If I could only choose one player from the last decade to build a team around, I'd have to choose Oscar Robertson. What do you think, Dennis," I said.

"Oscar is definitely one of the best, but the title of greatest player of all time goes to Wilt Chamberlain. In fact, Oscar Robertson called Wilt the Stilt the best player he ever played against! He's been the league MVP four times, and an All-Star more times than I can count. Did you know he once scored one hundred points in one game?"

"I did," I said. "Did you know they lost? It's your turn, Jackson."

"Pete Maravich is my choice. He has to be the most athletic player to ever play in the back court, no one else makes the passes he makes, behind the back, between the legs, and the no-look pass. Some people say he's a show-off, others say he's a hotdog or a ball hog. I say he has changed the game. It takes more than one man to guard him defensively, so teams have to use other players to help out, which creates openings for others to score. Take my word, if he's not the greatest player of all time now, he will be."

"Danny, you're next," I said.

"I'm choosing my father's favorite player, Elgin Baylor. I don't remember ever watching him play, but my father said he was the purest shooter he ever saw. My favorite player has always been Jerry West, and he described Elgin Baylor as the most spectacular player the game has ever known, and a role model for himself. If Jerry says he's that good, that's good enough for me."

Josh said, "I've seen highlights of Elgin Baylor, and he was spectacular, but I have to choose George Mikan. Before George, basketball was a small man's game, and the most desired skills were dribbling, passing, and shooting. Big men were too slow and uncoordinated to play the game until 6'10" George Mikan revolutionized the game. Suddenly, the lob pass and the offensive rebound became new strategies, and every team began scrambling to find someone who could defend him. He led the Boston Celtics to five straight NBA Championships."

"How do you know all that," Danny said.

"Because I played center in high school and our coach made us do all these drills called Mikan Drills, so one day, I asked him who Mikan was, and he told me all about him."

"That's cool," Thomas, said, "It sounds like every big man owes a debt of gratitude to George Mikan. I'm sure he was good, but as you said Josh, none of the other teams had a big man who could play against him. Today, every team has a big man and several of them are seven footers, so the competition is much greater today. Yet one player stands above them all, Kareem Abdul-Jabbar. He is the greatest professional basketball player of all time. If there's a record, he either owns it, or is on his way to breaking it. He is the King of Swat, with him in the paint, some teams don't even attempt an inside game. They even changed the college rules, prohibiting dunking the ball because it gave him too much of an advantage over the other players."

"It's time to vote and, remember, you can't vote for your own choice," I said. "When I call the names of those nominated, raise your hand if you think they are the greatest.

"How many for Maravich. No one, that's interesting.

"How about Robertson? No one again!

"Anyone for Chamberlain, I count two votes.

"Who's for Mikan, I see one vote.

"That leaves Baylor and Abdul-Jabbar, and there are three votes left, how many for Abdul-Jabbar, three votes.

"I had a feeling he might be the winner."

"Great choice, Thomas," Dennis said.

After playing the greatest game a second time, we all returned to either napping or visiting quietly with our seat companions.

Our first stop came at Junction City, Colorado, where several people transferred to other buses. Maria was one of the passengers who disembarked to catch another bus that would take her to Albuquerque, New Mexico. Dennis and I got off the bus to stretch our legs; we walked over to a nearby park, which had a statue in the center of it. The statue was of John Otto, the man responsible for the establishment of the Colorado National Monument in 1911. Its establishment protected the beautiful canyon lands of

Western Colorado. Otto, also known as the Hermit of the Canyons, single-handedly built many of the trails through the different canyons so people could experience the canyons up close and personal. The accompanying plaque also gave other information about the local area. Junction City takes its name from its location. It sits at the junction of the Colorado and Gunnison Rivers. The area was originally the home of the Ute Indians until white ranchers and farmers who homesteaded the area in the 1880s displaced them.

After the thirty-minute layover, our bus resumed its trek to Denver. For the next few hours, Dennis napped, and I completed crossword puzzles and word-finders in a paperback we bought at the Greyhound station in Junction City. It wasn't too long before you could feel the bus starting to climb as we made our way up the foothills of Rocky Mountains. Somewhere after we began climbing, I asked Josh, the cadet seated diagonally in front of me, if he liked attending the Air Force Academy.

He said, it's been good for him, not only the flight training, but the lifestyle experience as well. It had helped him focus his life and gave him a goal to achieve. He shared, "After my commitment to the Air Force is up, I plan on pursuing a career as an airline pilot. As I see it, I have the privilege of serving my country for five years, and in exchange, I get a college degree and five years of the best on-the-job training available, and they pay me while I'm learning. Most airline pilots who do not come out of the military take as long or longer to reach the same status as I'll have when my hitch is up. I think that's a pretty good deal!"

Josh asked, "What about you, what are your plans?"

"Well, I just graduated from high school this past June, and I will start college in a few weeks. I don't really have a profession in mind at this time; the only thing I know for sure is I'll be playing golf on the college golf team this spring. I'd like to be a professional golfer, but as my father says, it's always good to have a backup plan."

About this time, Dennis woke up, and asked if I knew any more mini-mysteries.

"I know several more," I said.

Dennis roused the troops and I explained how to play.

"A man lives on the seventeenth floor of his apartment building in New York City. He goes to the windows and looks out, looking in all directions. He then goes to the telephone, and makes several phone calls. He then returns to the windows to look again. After several minutes, he makes more phone calls. This time, he returns to the window and jumps out. On the way down, he realizes he didn't have to die. Why?"

"Was there anyone else in the room with him?" Jackson asked.

"No."

"Does looking out the windows have something to do with the answer?" Danny asked.

"Yes."

Dennis asked, "Are the phone calls important."

"Yes."

"Did he break up with his girlfriend, and that's why he jumped?" Thomas asked.

"No."

Josh asked, "Did something happen to make him jump?"

"Good question, yes!"

"Did someone die?" Thomas asked.

"Yes."

Dennis asked, "Did someone close to him die?"

"Yes."

"Did someone call him and tell him someone had died?" Dennis asked.

"No."

"When he called, did someone tell him someone died?" Danny asked.

"No."

"When he made the phone calls, did he talk to someone?" Jackson asked.

"No."

"No one," Josh said.

"Yes."

"Did a natural disaster happen, like a fire, or an earth-quake?" Dennis asked.

"That's more than one question," I said. "But the answers are, no and no."

"When he was looking out the windows, was he looking for someone?" Jackson asked.

"Yes."

"Someone specific," Josh asked.

"No."

"Did something happen that was not a natural disaster?" Dennis asked.

"Yes."

"Whatever the event was, did it cause him to jump?" Danny asked.

"Yes."

Jackson asked, "Was the event big?"

"Yes."

"Did the event destroy New York City?" Dennis asked.

"Yes!"

"Did a nuclear bomb go off?" Dennis asked.

"Yes!"

"I got it, I got it," Josh said. "A nuclear bomb went off and killed everyone."

"No, but you're on the right track."

"Were the people he called dead?" Jackson asked.

"Yes."

Dennis asked, "Did he think everyone was dead but him?"

"Yes!"

"I got it, really this time," Josh, said, "Everyone was killed by the nuclear bomb except him, so he jumped out the window, and on the way down, he changed his mind."

"Close," I said.

"You said the phone calls were important," Dennis said, "But no one answered his calls. Did someone call him?"

"No."

"Did he hear another phone ring after he jumped," asked Jackson.

"Yes, can you solve it!"

"He jumped out the window because he believed a nuclear bomb had killed everyone else, but on his way down, he hears a phone ringing and realizes he didn't have to die, someone besides himself was still alive."

"*Yes!*"

After we finished the mini-mystery, Dennis took out a deck of cards and we began playing spades. The cadets went back to their own conversation. After we played spades, we played hearts, and lastly, gin rummy. After losing three games in a row, I was tired of cards, and I went back to crossword puzzles. While I sulked—I hate losing—Dennis struck up a conversation with Jackson, and they began talking about history, and the cool things about Colorado Springs.

Jackson said, "The most interesting events happen at Pikes Peak, which is about ten miles west of Colorado Springs; it's named for Zebulon Pike who led an expedition to Southern Colorado in 1806. There's the Pikes Peak International Hill Climb, where cars race each other up the twisting and winding road to the top, and there's the grueling Pikes Peak Marathon where runners run to the top. Of course, Colorado Springs is where the Air Force Academy is located. Though you can't get close to it, nearby is NORAD, the North America Air Defense Command located inside Cheyenne Mountain. Colorado Springs is also home to the Cheyenne Mountain Zoo and Pioneers Museum. Most of the founding fathers made their fortunes by striking it rich in the gold fields near Cripple Creek. General William Palmer, who is considered the founder of Colorado Springs, used a great deal of his fortune to build the Antlers Hotel which is still a major attraction today."

We arrived in Denver a few minutes before 7:00 p.m. We said our good-byes to the cadets, collected our belongings, and headed across the street to get something to eat. As we ate our meal, Dennis laid out the evening plan for me.

"Since we are not near the ocean anymore," he said, "and there aren't any public beaches in Colorado as far as I know, the next best place to stay is at a rest stop. They have restrooms, and some have showers and fire pits. Tomorrow, we'll head north to Loveland, it's about an hour from here, and we can stay tomorrow night at Boyd Lake."

We finished dinner, and before we left, we both made telephone calls from a public pay phone. I called my parents to let them know our location, and to let them know we'd be heading back home in a few days. Dennis called Austin to get an update on the strike. It was nearly 8:00 p.m., and we probably had no more than hour before the sunset below the Rocky Mountains, so we walked briskly to the nearest on ramp to I-25 headed north. After fifteen minutes, we had not secured a ride, so we decided to start walking.

Dennis said, "I'm sure there's a rest stop a few miles out of town."

We walked maybe a half-mile and to my surprise, I could see a sign that read "Rest stop one mile."

I started to lay my bedding out when Dennis said, "You might want to move further away from the brush so the rattlesnakes don't get you."

I grabbed my tarp, and pulled it across the parking lot to the green grass near the restroom. When I looked back, Dennis was still standing there, laughing. He called me back and said it would be all right. He might have been joking, but I wasn't sure.

"I hate snakes," I said, "With their forked tongues flicking in and out of their mouths. I understand that's how they smell, but I don't like it. We had a school assembly once, and as we came into the gym, there were several gunnysacks lying by the wall, you could see something moving inside them, someone said they were snakes, and I made the mistake of saying I hated snakes. When they asked for volunteers, my so-called high school friends began shouting my name. To prove I wasn't chicken, I volunteered. The man brought over one of the gunnysacks, opened it up, and pulled out a three-foot-long Egyptian Lizard. The forked tongue on it was ten times the size of a snake's, and it flicked it at me throughout the whole assembly. I hate snakes and lizards too."

We settled in for the evening as cars and trucks came and went. As we talked, Dennis explained a little more about his friend we were going to visit. "His name is Jack," he said, "We were stationed together on the same base in Germany." Jack was an MP, which stands for military police, and they were both on their second tour of duty, having both spent their first tour in Vietnam. They hit it off right away, and eventually they shared an apartment together as part of on-base housing. They also spent their time off exploring West Germany's nightlife.

Dennis said after getting out of the army in 1967, he had spent several weeks visiting with Jack and his family in Loveland, but except for a few letters, he hadn't had any contact with them since then. As Dennis talked, I could see how much he was looking forward to seeing Jack again, and catching up on the news from the last seven years.

I asked Dennis what the nightlife was like in Germany.

He said, "There's a lot of small clubs near the base that the GIs frequent, the beer is cheap, the music is loud, and there are plenty of young girls looking for a good time. Drugs are common, but you had to be careful. Being drunk would get you thrown in the brig, but being caught with drugs would get you court-martialed. Jack refused to be around anyone who used drugs, so I stayed away from them mostly during my tour in Germany."

Since we were discussing drug use, and I always wanted to know why Dennis used drugs. I decided to take the opportunity to ask.

I said, "Why would you use drugs when they're so bad for you?"

Dennis closed his eyes, and then he said, "Americans have been brainwashed about drugs."

He said, "You like soda pop, right, did you know it has the drug caffeine in it? The same drug is found in coffee. Why do you think three quarters of Americans have to have a cup of coffee in the morning so they can wake up?

You know my dad smokes. Did you know that the U. S. government gave cigarettes to soldiers during WWI and WWII, and encouraged them to smoke? Tobacco has the drug nicotine in it, and most smokers can't quit because they're addicted to it."

Dennis continued, "In the center of our brain there is a place called the pleasure center, and all our senses are connected to it, so when we see, hear, smell, or taste something we like, the pleasure center remembers it, and we become attracted to the sensation because it makes us feel good. Pot and other drugs illicit the same response from the pleasure center of the brain and people continue to use them because they're enjoyable. The only reason why marijuana is illegal in America is the big tobacco and alcohol companies don't want more competition. If you look at the record of which members of congress supported marijuana being classified as an illegal drug, or who introduces more bills to spend money to put more cops on the street to arrest drug dealers and drug users. You will find they are the congressmen from the States with big ties to tobacco and alcohol."

I said, "So you don't think drugs are bad for you, or that using some drugs leads to using other drugs?"

"I didn't say that," he said, "I'm just trying to point out people eat foods like chocolate, or listen to music because they stimulate our pleasure centers, and there are many drugs we accept and we don't question their use. People need to realize that propaganda supported by the greed of several American corporations has more to do with the public's opinion about certain drugs, than the negative effects the drugs might have."

"So you think we should legalize drugs like heroin and LSD," I said.

"No, but I do think drugs such as pot and cocaine are no more dangerous than alcohol, and it's legal for those over the age of twenty-one."

"You do know why the legal age to drink is twenty-one," I said.

"Because you're considered an adult, and you can think for yourself by then," Dennis said.

"That's true, but also because your liver is fully developed by the age of twenty-one, and can process alcohol quicker so your body is less affected by the poison. What about the evidence pot smokers have less motivation and become more lethargic the longer they smoke marijuana," I said.

Dennis retorted, "Pot is no worse than tobacco."

"What's your response to the Bible verse that says our body is God's Temple, and we should treat it as such," I said.

"I'm not sure if that verse is talking about our physical bodies or our spiritual bodies, but let's just say it is talking about our physical bodies. Then maybe we shouldn't consume so much sugar that our teeth rot and decay."

I didn't want the evening to end on such a sour note, so I suggested we play The Greatest Game.

Dennis said, "What's the greatest invention of all time?"

I took a few minutes to think before I spoke, "Several things come to mind, the combustion engine, the cotton gin, the phonograph, but I'd have to say the greatest invention of all time is the lightbulb. The lightbulb changed the world; people were no longer dependent on sunlight for illumination. Factories could now stay open longer during the shorter daylight months or even add a second shift. Street lamps provided merchants greater opportunities as communities lit downtown streets. The lightbulb changed how we spend our evenings and night time hours."

"I'd agree," Dennis, said, "The lightbulb is one of the greatest inventions, but not the greatest. I'd rank the telephone, and the airplane higher than the lightbulb, but I say the greatest invention of all time has to be the television. The telephone ushered in the electronics age, and suddenly the world became smaller, you could pick up a phone and talk to your neighbor down the street or a relative halfway across the country without leaving your home. The airplane made the world even smaller by making travel faster. Today, it only takes hours to reach places it used to take days, weeks, or months. However, the television has allowed us to go places and see things without leaving our living rooms. We get almost instant information, with pictures, of events from around the world on the evening news. If the light-bulb changed the culture of how we spend our evenings, then TV has revolutionized our culture itself."

I said, "I agree, one point for you! But I still think I'm ahead in total points."

As I closed my eyes, I kept having visions of snakes and lizards, and every time I heard a noise, I jumped. It was long night.

— 11 —

THE NEXT MORNING, we got up a little later than usual, but we were able to catch a ride to the Loveland exit quickly. The town is located off the freeway, so we walked into town and made our first stop the local diner for breakfast. As we sat and ate our pancakes with peanut butter and maple syrup, Dennis told me a little more about his friend Jack and Jack's family. He said Jack's mother, Willow, is a saint; she makes everyone feel like family. Jack's father passed away when he was young, and Willow raised Jack by herself. She worked two and sometimes three jobs to put clothes on his back, food on the table, and a roof over their heads. Willow not only raised Jack, but also a cousin named Kit, whose parents tragically died in a car accident when she was nine.

Dennis said, "Kit was a college student the last time I was here." We finished breakfast and then made our daily phone call to get the update on the strike. Austin said both sides had agreed to mediation. The next step would be agreeing on a mediator from a list, and that should happen in the next couple of days.

By now, it was nearly 9:00 a.m., so Dennis and I headed off to Jack's mother's home to see if we could find were Jack might be. We knocked on Willow's door, and a few moments later, a woman wearing a yellow cotton bathrobe and matching slippers opened the door. She reminded me of the grandmotherly type, who hugged you as if you've plopped face down into a waterbed. She looked at me first with no reaction, but when she looked at Dennis, a big smile spread across her face, and as she rushed to give him a big hug, her reading glasses fell off her head. I picked up her glasses and followed the two of them as she took Dennis's hand and led him into the living room then raced to the kitchen and returned with three cups of coffee.

Being polite, I accepted a cup even though I don't drink the stuff. Dennis introduced me, and I said, "Dennis speaks fondly of your family."

She said, "Jack's going to be so excited to see you, he's not married, but he does have a nice girlfriend, and they have a house near the edge of town. Both Jack and Kit talk about you now and then; Kit teaches elementary school in Greeley, but lives here in town. How long are you going to be here for?"

Dennis said, "Just today. We need to continue on home tomorrow."

"Well you're always welcome here," Willow said, "I've got extra beds."

Dennis asked, "Do you still have the property out at the lake?"

Willow said, "Oh my, yes, it's been in our family for three generations, and when I pass on, it will go to Jack. Feel free to stay out there if you'd like, but you have to at least eat supper here."

Dennis said, "It's a deal."

"Jack usually checks in with me each morning," Willow said. "And when he calls, I'll let him know you're headed out to the lake."

As we left, she said, "I'll expect you for dinner around 5:00 p.m., we're having chicken and dumplings."

As we left the house, Dennis said, "Boyd Lake is just a few miles away." So we started walking. He said, "I have a lot fond memories of swimming and hanging out at this lake with Jack and Kit and some of their friends. By the time we get there, the temperature will be warm enough to go swimming." After walking a couple of miles, we turned and headed down a narrow tree-lined gravel road. It was as if we were under a canopy out of sight from the summer sun. As we continued, I could hear a fast-approaching vehicle. Startled, I turned quickly when I heard the sound of a siren. As a cold wave surged through my body, I froze. I thought to myself, *Did we do something wrong, are we trespassing?*

The deputy sheriff's car slammed to a stop just a few feet from where I was standing, the driver's side door opened, and a tall, muscular man got out. He said, "What are you doing here?" I turned and looked at Dennis.

He said, "We're going skinny dipping, do you want to join us?"

Not knowing how to react, I just stood there like a stone, watching as the deputy approached Dennis. And when I thought he was about to handcuff him, he grabbed him and gave him a bear hug. After the officer put Dennis down, I still stood there completely frozen. Then Dennis said, "Jack, this is my cousin, Nathan."

I said, "This is Jack!"

Dennis laughed. "Yeah, didn't I tell you he was deputy sheriff?"

We got in Jack's car, and he drove us the rest of the way to the lake. The place was like a finely manicured park; the grass was lush and green and ran right out to the edge of the water. There was an old cabin that had obviously seen better days and a rope swing that swung out over the lake. The next thing I knew, they were both stripping down to their skivvies and running for the lake. Dennis grabbed the rope and swung out into the lake and let go. Jack followed suit. Not to be left behind, I joined in the frivolity. After several jumps, we collapsed on the green grass and just lay there, soaking up the sun. After a while, Jack got up and put his uniform back on and went to his car. Dennis followed him and the two began talking. I figured I'd give them some time to catch up on what had happened since the last time they had seen each other and took a few more swings on the rope.

When they returned to the lake, Dennis and Jack had more somber looks on their faces. Dennis said, "Jack's going to give us a ride to Kit's place, and then he'll pick us up and bring us back out here in a few hours."

When we arrived at Kit's house, a young woman with a child came out to greet us. Kit was beautiful, blonde-haired, blue-eyed, with a curvy body. Her daughter, Casey, was a spitting image of her mother, very angelic. After a short greeting, we all went inside where Kit and Casey served us ice tea. I hate ice tea, but being polite, I graciously accepted it. Jack finished his glass and said, that he had to get back to work, but he'd be back to pick us up. As he walked away, I could see the outline of his wet underwear beneath his uniform, and I thought to myself, *I hope he doesn't have to do anything in the line duty before his shorts dry.*

Shortly after Jack left, Kit and Dennis went into another room. I could hear them whispering, and figured it was none of my business, so I asked Casey if she had a favorite book I could read to her. She said, "Yes," and went to retrieve it. As she returned, we both could clearly hear the whispers in the other room had turned to sobbing. Casey said, "My mom does that a lot, she's very sad. I think it's because the doctors say I'm going to die. I have leukemia.

"I try to tell her it will be okay, God will take care of me, but I still hear her crying every night."

I could feel my face go flush and the palms of my hands were clammy. It felt like someone had just punched me in the stomach, or stabbed me in the heart with a knife, but when I looked at Casey and how calm she was, all I could say was, "You're a very brave little girl."

She looked at me and said, "When it hurts, I just try and think about how beautiful heaven will be."

I couldn't stop the tears from welling up in my eyes as I started to read.

The Star Tree

There once was a young fir tree, which stood at the edge of the woods. Since her days as a seedling, she had grown tall and straight under the watchful eye of her mother, which stood like a giant of the forest just a few limbs' length away.

It was spring and the trees of the forest were all celebrating the birth of new life. The cones that had fallen from their bows last fall were now sprouting as new seedlings.

In the past, the young fir tree had watched as other trees produced cones that gave birth to new trees, but this would be her first year to bear cones, and she was filled with excitement.

As buds formed on her bows, she counted them. First, there were three, then nine, and finally, she counted twenty buds, that would grow into fir cones.

Throughout the spring and summer, the young tree nurtured her cones, and they grew big and healthy. As fall arrived, their color began to change from green to a light-brown color as they soon would begin to drop from her branches.

One, then two, then four of the young tree's cones fell. Within a few days, half of her cones had fallen near the base of her roots. But before the rest of her cones could fall, a strong windstorm blew through the forest.

The young tree's limbs where twisted and tossed in every direction as the windstorm shook her from top to bottom. Her remaining cones flew off her bows like missiles in all directions. The young tree was able to follow only one small cone's flight, which took it out into the field bordering the woods. She had no idea of the others' final destination.

As the approach of winter drew closer, the animals of the forest gathered the last stores of food they would need to survive through the harsh winter months. The young tree's heart sank as she watched several squirrels gather up all the cones around her feet and carry them off to their den.

The young tree's hopes of becoming a mother tree now rested on one small cone lying in the open field beyond the tree line of the woods.

As spring arrived and seedlings began to break through the golden earth of the forest, the young tree watched to see if her cone that had landed in the open field had spouted, but her view was obstructed by the low grass that covered the ground.

Weeks passed and just as the young tree was about to abandon hope, the small green nose of a seedling pushed its way above the height of the field grass. At this sight, the newest mother tree of the forest held her limbs up a little higher.

The new mother knew her young seedling would have to overcome many obstacles to survive. Most new seedlings are protected by their mother against the harsh elements, but because of the distance between herself and the new seedling, she would not be able to provide shelter from the blistering summer sun, nor from the ice and snow of winter.

As the seasons passed and the seedling became a young tree, it was clear to her, and the rest of the forest trees, the seedling's growth lagged far behind the level of the other young trees. Some of other trees had even started calling the young tree a bush rather than a tree.

By the age of four, most of the young trees of the woods were well over four feet tall and were beginning to fill out nicely. However, the Little Field Tree, as it had been nicknamed, stood barely two feet tall and was very scrawny compared to other trees its age. While other mother trees bragged about their offspring, the mother of the Little Field Tree said nothing to the other trees, but reassured her young tree she loved her, and unlike the other trees of the forest, the Little Tree was special.

One day, the children of the owners of the field came and cleaned the weeds away from the Little Field Tree's roots. After which they brought a bucket of water to feed it. They continued bringing water each day throughout the summer to help it grow stronger. When Christmas came, they brought red bows and stars made from tinfoil to decorate the Little Field Tree.

The Little Field Tree's mother no longer remained silent when other mothers talked of their offspring, instead she now bragged how lovely her young tree looked and started referring to it as "The Star Tree."

A tradition was born, and each Christmas, the children came and decorated the Star Tree. Then one year, the family who owned the field sold it and moved away. The other trees of the forest, who were jealous of the attention the Star Tree had received in the past, now began to taunt the Star Tree, saying, "Who's going to decorate you now!"

As the Christmas season arrived, the trees of the woods waited to see if someone would come and decorate the Star Tree, but no one came.

Christmas Eve morning began with a cloudy sky, but by afternoon, the clouds had disappeared, and the sky was a light-colored blue, which meant it would be a cool, clear evening. As the sun began to set, any hope the Star Tree had of being decorated seem to have disappeared.

Then, to the amazement of all, as the evening sky burst forth with a spectacular show of a brilliant lights, the Star Tree began to twinkle, as if nature had attached hundreds of stars to its bows, and crowned it with the Evening Star, which shone brightest of all.

From that night on, every Christmas Eve, the stars of the heavens aligned themselves to decorate the Star Tree, for as her mother had always said, she was special!

When I was finished, Casey said, "That's my favorite book. I've outgrown most of my other children's books, but I think I will always keep this one."

Dennis and Kit returned from the other room just as Casey finished speaking. Kit's eyes were obviously red from crying. We all looked at each other, but no one said a word. Then Casey cut the dark, awkward silence with the words, "Can we have a picnic in the backyard?"

Kit said, "I think that's a wonderful idea."

Jack picked us up in his deputy sheriff's car, as promised, and took us back out to the lake. As he left, he said, "I'll pick you up around four-thirty. Mom's expecting us for dinner at five."

Back at the lake, Dennis remained somber. He said, "You know, for a few weeks several years ago, I actually laid here staring out at this lake, and I forgot about the war and believed real joy was possible." I wasn't sure if he was talking about the Vietnam War, or the war going on inside him, but I had an idea of what he meant by joy. I left Dennis to his thoughts and went to play on the rope swing for a while. When I returned, I sat down on the soft green grass next to Dennis. He said, "Have you ever wished you could go back in time and change what you've done, and start your life from that point again?" He looked at me and said, "Of course you haven't. You're only eighteen, but a day will come when you'll wish you could."

Right on schedule, Jack returned to pick us up, this time in his private car. Along with Jack was his girlfriend Renee. Jack introduced her to us, and we exchanged pleasantries before leaving for Willow's for dinner. When we got there, Kit and Casey were there as well. Willow said, "I thought as long as I was going to cook for five, I might as well cook for seven."

Willow sat at the head of the table with Jack and Renee on her right. Casey sat next to Willow on her left, followed by myself and Kit. Dennis sat next to Kit at the other end of the table. After Jack said grace, we each passed our plates, and Willow dished up bountiful portions of her chicken and dumplings. As the small talk began, I ate and listened. Jack shared his most exciting experience as a deputy sheriff, the capture of two bank robbers who had robbed a bank in Denver and then fled north. The suspects decided to take the Loveland exit in the hope of finding a place to hide, only to find Jack and another fellow deputy waiting for them.

Renee talked about how she met Jack. "While reading the power meter at a rural home, I discovered an indoor pot-growing operation. The officer responding to the call was Jack." That was two years ago. Kit talked about school, Dennis talked about our stay in San Francisco, and Willow tried prying information from Dennis about his love life. What no one mentioned was anything about Casey and her illness.

After dinner, we retired to the living room where Willow served pecan pie, which I hate, but I accepted it graciously. After another hour of small talk, we said our good-byes, which included big, smothering hugs from Willow. I thanked her for dinner and the pie. Then we all crowded into Jack's car, including Kit and Casey, and drove to their family cabin on the lake. The evening temperature was still near eighty degrees so we went swimming again, even Casey. I was surprised Kit let her go swimming being so ill. After a while, Kit wrapped Casey up in a towel, and they both went and sat with Renee, who wasn't swimming. Jack, Dennis, and I continued to play. Sometime later, Dennis got out, and he and Kit took a long walk along the lake. Before they returned, Jack had a small fire built, and the rest of us were roasting marshmallows.

As the fire burned down to embers, Jack said they had to leave, but he would return in the morning. As we said our good-byes, I could see the same sadness returning to Kit's eyes as I had seen in Dennis's eyes earlier in the day. I thought to myself, *Joy can be such a fleeting thing*. As the others lingered by the car, I placed a few more pieces of wood in the fire, and as they pulled away, I waved good-bye. Dennis returned to the fire, and as we sat quietly for a few minutes, I could hear the sound of a frog croaking, the high-pitched whine of a mosquito buzzing around my head, but not the thoughts of Dennis.

With the moon nearly full, the reflection off the lake seemed to illuminate the cabin site.

I said, "They are nice people. I'm glad we came this way."

Dennis said, "They certainly are. I had forgotten how much I enjoyed their company."

"It's sad about Casey," I said. To which there was no response.

"Do you know who her father is?"

"Someone Kit met in college."

Dennis said, "It's been a long day."

I said, good night to Dennis and closed my eyes. I was suddenly homesick.

The early morning sunlight crept through the trees and surrounded the cabin like a thief, intent on stealing my sleep. I awoke to find Dennis already packed and ready to leave. He said, "Hurry up. Jack will be here soon to take us to breakfast." After I finished packing, I took a walk around, trying to cement the images of this place in my mind. I had no camera, just the film in my head, so I took a little extra time to process the pictures. Some places are more than special, and you never want to forget how they look, or how you felt while you were there.

Jack arrived and we jumped into his car. We sped down the old gravel road until we reached the county highway. As we drove through town, we passed the streets on which Willow and Kit lived, I said a silent good-bye. A few min-

utes later, we arrived at the Junction Restaurant. As Jack and
Dennis waited for a booth, I told Dennis to order the usual
for me. I then made my way to the public phone booth and
called Austin to see if there was any news about the strike.
He said, "The union and company had agreed on a mediator and the first meeting was scheduled for tomorrow." He
wasn't sure how long it would take to completely work out
the details of a new contract, but he expected there could
be something for the union members to vote on in three
or four days. I then made a phone call home to talk to my
mom; I guess I just needed to hear her voice.

When I sat down to eat, I gave Dennis the latest news
on the strike. As I ate, I listened to Jack and Dennis making plans for Jack and Renee to come to Longview next
summer. Jack said, "Maybe I'll make it part of a honey-
moon trip." When they finished, I asked Dennis what's our
next destination.

"Home," he said, "by the way of the Great Salt Lake."

Jack said, "It's about five hundred miles from here to
Salt Lake City."

Dennis said, "I'd like to stay the night on Antelope
Island, if we can cover the miles."

"Cool," I said. "I've never been to the Great Salt Lake."

As we said good-bye, Jack and Dennis shook hands,
and then gave each other hugs. As we made our way to
the freeway on ramp to start hitchhiking, Dennis watched

Jack drive off. It was about 7:30 a.m. I couldn't help but think about Jack and Dennis's friendship and how strong it remains, even though they hadn't seen each other in years. I wondered if it was a product of the time spent together during the war or something else. I guess what I struggled with most was trying to think of a friend I was that close with.

— 12 —

WE WERE AT the on-ramp only a few minutes when a middle-aged man in a pea-green Ford pickup with a generator in the back pulled over. We ran up to his truck in hopes of getting a ride. He asked us where we were headed; we told him Salt Lake City. He said he could give us a ride as far as Interstate 80. So we hopped in.

We introduced ourselves, and he said his name was Charlie. He was wearing tan overalls, with a tan Carhartt jacket. I asked him where he was headed, and he said Cheyenne, Wyoming. He said he worked for an oil company and did routine maintenance on the company's oil wells. Today, he was on his way to work on two wells near Cheyenne. Dennis asked Charlie what he liked best about his job. Charlie said, "It's different every day."

I asked, "What's the worst part?"

He replied, "Winter and travel. It gets cold around here, and it never fails. The colder it gets, the more problems we have. I call it job security."

Charlie asked if we'd ever been to the Cheyenne Frontier Days, to which we both replied no. He said, "That's too bad. You don't know what you're missing. It's the second largest rodeo in America. All the best cowboys are here as well as the best acts in country music. It's a weeklong party."

"I know Cheyenne is a large city now," I said, "But what brought people to the area originally?"

"Cheyenne was plotted by the Union Pacific Railroad during construction of the Transcontinental Railroad," Charlie said. "It soon became a shipping hub and a market for cattle. During the early 1900s oil was discovered in the region, and soon, refineries and pipelines followed which reshaped the community, but cows and cowboys are its heritage."

Dennis asked Charlie what his favorite rodeo event was. He said, "My favorite is calf roping. I like the speed of the calves as they sprint out the gate, the sound of the lariat as it swirls above your head before you throw it, watching the loop in the rope as it tightens around the back legs of the calf. My brother-in-law and I like to enter a few of the local rodeos around here each year, and we even win a few bucks now and then." Charlie then asked if we had a favorite event.

Dennis said, "My favorite is the bull riding, it might be short in length, but it's extremely exciting to watch as the bull turns and spins. I don't know how a rider can stay on. The front of the bull is going one direction, and the back end of the bull is going the opposite direction. Bull riders are more than cowboys. They're great athletes."

I said, "I like the bull riding and the calf roping, but I love the bucking broncos best. I once saw a rider get bucked ten feet into the air."

"Really," Charlie said.

"Well maybe not ten feet, but it looked like it," I said. "I'm always afraid the riders are going to get their hand caught in the rope they tie around the horn of the saddle. I've seen several riders dragged by their horses and get stepped on when they fall off."

"It's definitely not a sport for the faint of heart," Charlie said.

I asked Charlie if he'd ever been to the Ellensburg Rodeo.

He said he'd heard of it but had never been there.

I said, "It's the only rodeo I've ever been to, but I've been to it several times, and every time, I have fun. I've always loved the rodeo clowns the best."

Dennis asked Charlie if he was a big country and western music fan. "Definitely, yes," he said.

"Well Dennis and I have a game we play while we're hitchhiking, it's called The Greatest Game, we each pick who is the greatest at something. So my question is, Who's the greatest country and western singer of all time? Do you want to play?"

"Sure," he said.

"Who wants to go first?" I said.

"I'll go first," Charlie said.

"My favorite singer is Merle Haggard, but I don't think there's any doubt the greatest country singer of all time is Johnny Cash. He has that low, raspy voice, which is maybe not the greatest, but combined with the songs he sings and his delivery, it's pure country. He has to have more number one hits than anyone else."

I said, "I think you're probably right about the number one hits, but I don't think having the most number one hits makes someone necessarily the greatest country singer of all time. My father's favorites are Hank Snow, Johnny Cash, and Charlie Pride, but as far as who has the best voice, my choice is Jim Reeves, easily. His voice is a hot knife cutting through butter, so smooth, it flows like a beautiful stream. I could listen to it all day. What do you think, Dennis?"

"When I think about someone who's the greatest, I think about someone who has set the standard everyone after them follows, and that could only be Hank Williams. He recorded more songs than any other country singer of his time did, and his style is as relevant today as it was thirty years ago. Hank is true legend."

"All right, it's time to vote," Dennis said, "Would anyone like to switch their choice?"

"I would," I said, "I still think that Jim Reeves has the best voice, but I think Johnny Cash is clearly the greatest country singer of all time. Just look at how many decades his career and hits cover."

"I guess that makes you the winner, Charlie," Dennis said. "Unless you're going to change your vote."

As we reached the intersection of Highways 25 and 80, Charlie pulled over to let us out. It had been a quick trip; Charlie had a bit of a lead foot. I had noticed several times the speedometer had passed the eighty-five-miles-per-hour mark and was consistently at the eighty-miles-per-hour mark throughout the drive. The funny thing is we were being passed by other vehicles most of the trip. I thought to myself, *I guess the government's mandatory fifty-five-miles-per-hour speed limit doesn't apply in Colorado and Wyoming.* We thanked Charlie for the ride and watched as he sped off.

As we waited for a ride that would take us west toward Salt Lake City, I asked Dennis about the place we were going to camp at. He said, "It's called Antelope Island, and it's one of several islands in the Great Salt Lake. It's named after the antelope that live there, but the island is also home to a small herd of bison. The last time I was there, it had the nicest facilities on the lake, with clean places to camp, good access to the lake for going swimming, restrooms with showers, which are a necessity for washing the salt off your body after you swim, and a seasonal restaurant."

A car pulled up and asked us where we were headed, but since they were not going more than a few miles, we thanked them for stopping, but passed on the ride. About fifteen minutes later, a Chevy van stopped. They said they were headed to Evanston, Wyoming, which would take us more than half the way to our destination, so we climbed in. The van was packed with climbing gear, two bicycles, and a mattress, no rear seats, so we climbed onto the mattress and made ourselves comfortable. The sides of the van were covered in orange-and-red colored shag carpet, and it smelled faintly of wet dog.

The young couple introduced themselves as Mike and Becky. Mike was all arms and legs, with a burnt-red beard. He said, "We're headed for the Mirror Lake Scenic Byway for an eighty-mile back road adventure between Evanston, Wyoming, and Kamas, Utah."

Becky, who had the voice of a cheerleader, said, "Along the way, we also plan to do some hiking and bike riding, as we explore the Uinta Mountains and Wasatch-Cache National Forest."

We introduced ourselves, and Dennis explained we were headed to Antelope Island where we planned to spend the night and go swimming in the Great Salt Lake. I shared we had hitch-hiked Highway 101 along the Oregon and California Coast to San Francisco, and from there to Reno, we had visited friends in Loveland, Colorado, and were now headed back home to Washington State.

Mike said, "They were from Kearney, Nebraska, and were taking an extended weekend trip." He pulled out some eight-track tapes of Aerosmith, Pink Floyd, ZZ Top, Led Zeppelin, and Deep Purple and asked what we wanted to listen to. Dennis said, "Pink Floyd," so Mike put in "Dark Side of the Moon" and proceeded to turn up the volume and rock us out.

We measured the distance between Cheyenne and Evanston not in miles but in eight-track tapes, we covered the distance in ZZ Top's "Rio Grande Mud," Led Zeppelin's "House of the Holy," Aerosmith's "Get Your Wings," Deep Purple's "Machine Head," The Eagles' "Desperado," Blue Oyster Cult's "Blue Oyster Cult," The Who's "Who's Next" and Pink Floyd's "Dark Side of the Moon" again. Somewhere in Aerosmith's tape, I drifted off, and the next thing I remember, Deep Purple was playing. Mike and Becky didn't have much to say, not even to each other, but they sang all the words to nearly every song. It made me wonder how many times they had played those tapes. My tapes always seem to last about a year before they fall apart. As we arrived in Evanston, Mike turned off the eight-track stereo, the blaring noise disappeared, but the ringing in my ears continued. As we said our good-byes, I thought to myself of all the people we have traveled with, I know the least about these two, except they liked their music loud.

According to my figures, there was about another ninety miles to our destination. It was now 2:30 p.m., so I estimated we should reach Antelope Island sometime between 4:00 p.m. and 5:00 p.m. if we caught a ride in the next fifteen-twenty minutes. Our next ride came from two young men in an older blue Toyota Corolla. They were dressed in black slacks, white pressed shirts with ties, and they introduced themselves as Elder Zack and Elder Francis. They said they were on their way to Salt Lake City on church business, but we were welcome to ride along. Dennis and I looked at each other and then climbed onto the back seat. For a second, I thought we may have made a mistake, but then I remembered rule number four: any ride is better than walking.

My concerns about accepting the ride were quickly realized. As we pulled onto the freeway, the first question Francis asked us was if we were fellow members of the, "Church of Latter Day Saints?" To which I replied no. Zack then explained that he and Francis were getting ready to go on their two-year mission to spread the Gospel of Jesus Christ. I said, "I believe in Jesus Christ, but I don't think we believe the same thing." Thinking that this might be a very short ride if this discussion became to argumentative, I decided it was better to express my faith than to be concerned whether or not they continued to give us a ride.

I asked, "Who is Jesus Christ in your faith?"

Zach said, "Jesus was chosen, according to the Gospels, to die for our sins so that we might have salvation."

I said, "According to the Gospels, Jesus is the Son of God, is that what you believe?"

"Yes," said Francis, "He is the firstborn son of God."

"So does God have other children?" Dennis asked.

"Satan," Francis said.

"Where do you find that in the Bible?" I asked.

"I'm not sure," said Francis, "But we believe all spiritual entities that existed prior to the creation of humans are brothers and sisters because they all came from God."

"So you don't believe there's a difference between angels and the Son of God," I said.

There was no response, so I asked, "What's the difference between the Bible and the Book of Mormon?"

Zach said, "The Book Mormon is an addition to the Bible, in the early 1800s, God sent Joseph Smith a vision, and anointed him a prophet with the purpose of restoring the Christian Church, which had turned away from Him. God then gave Joseph Smith new revelations he wrote down and compiled as the Book of Mormon."

I asked Zach, "Is your faith based upon the Bible or the Book of Mormon?"

"Both," said Zach. "The Bible is our original book, but the Book of Mormon gives us greater understanding of God and his will."

Dennis spoke up, "What do you know about Joseph Smith? Did you know he was a con man who stole people's money by claiming he could find buried treasure by using magical seer stones? That he was a polygamist who believed that it was acceptable to build his so-called church through sexual exploitation of women in the same way some slave masters increased the number of their slaves, by fathering children with the slave women and girls they owned? That anytime someone disagreed with his decrees, he either kicked him or her out of the congregation, or claimed God had given him a new vision, and changed the original decree. If you've studied the Old Testament prophets, does this sound like any of them? Did you know the Bible says the penalty for false prophecy is death?"

As Dennis blew through his accusations and history lesson, I watched Zach and Francis's faces, I was sure we would soon be left by the side of the road to find ourselves another ride, but instead they smiled and kept on driving. They had obviously been taught not argue with nonbelievers, but instead choose to see all attacks against them as persecution from an unbelieving world. Not wanting to ruffle their feathers too much more, I ask if I could ask a few more questions, to which they agreed, if they could ask a few questions when I was through.

I asked if Joseph Smith was Jewish.

To which they said, "No."

"Would you agree that in the Old Testament, God sent prophets to speak to His people, which are the Jewish people?"

To which they said, "Yes."

"Do you believe Jesus came to the earth to be the Messiah of the Jews, but they rejected Him?"

"Yes," they said.

"Do you believe through Jesus's crucifixion, Jesus completed God's plan for salvation?"

To which they shook their heads. "Yes."

"Did Jesus, who is the Son of God, not teach His disciples everything about God's plan for salvation, and how we should to treat one another?"

To which they replied, "Yes," once more.

"Do you believe the disciples were inspired by God to record Jesus's teaching as God's Holy Word?"

To which they answered, "Yes," in unison.

"So why would God need to send another prophet after Jesus completed all the Bible's prophecies concerning the Messiah, and more importantly, God's plan of salvation?"

Francis answered, "Because God had a new message."

Before I could speak again, Dennis broke in, saying, "What do you do with the verse in Revelation that says let no man add or take away from God's Word, and if you do, you will suffer plagues or be removed from the Book of Life!"

I was taken back completely by Dennis's ferocity and his passion. I wasn't sure how to take it, did he just want to set these young men straight for argument's sake? Or did he really feel he needed to speak to them as a man of God about their errant beliefs? Moreover, if it was as a man of God, what had brought about this sudden change of heart?

I said, "I've asked all my questions, do you have any questions for me?"

As they sat in the front seat, staring out the windshield, I could see they were thinking, especially Zach, who was driving, but neither asked a question or made another comment. I thought to myself, *Should I say more or not?* I wondered if this was the first time someone had brought up questions about their faith they hadn't encountered before. Would our discourse cause them to think, or to seek the answers to our questions, or only reinforce their false teachings?

After a few minutes, Zach asked if they could drive us to Antelope Island State Park. I said, "If it's not a burden, I know we'd appreciate it." As they dropped us off at the park entrance, we thanked them for the ride. As we departed, Francis handed us a Mormon Tract. I couldn't help but say one more thing as they left, "Read the Bible. It's the true Word of God, and if you do, God will reveal Himself to you."

As Dennis and I entered the park, he pointed to the trail he said we wanted to take. After we had walked a quarter mile or so, we came to a rustic camping area with a restroom and showers. We chose a spot and laid out our packs and changed into our swimsuits. Dennis said, "You'll want to keep your tennis shoes on so you don't cut your feet on the rubbish scattered along the bottom of the lake." He said, "When we get out waist deep, you can just lay back and relax. You will just float, it's so cool." We made our way down the slope from the campground onto a sandy beach; at least I thought it was, until I noticed the sand moving. Upon closer inspection, I was grossed out by what appeared to be millions of bugs the size of sand granules repeatedly crawling over the top of each other.

Upon entering the water Dennis said, "Don't swallow any water, and keep it out your eyes if you don't want them to sting." We walked out from the shore for what seemed like forever before we finally reached a depth deep enough to lie down and float. It was well worth crossing the beach of bugs and wading several hundred yards into the lake. I'd never experienced such exhilarating freedom, without any movement, you just float. After floating for several minutes, I looked up into the blue, blue, sky, it was almost dreamlike. I don't think I'd ever been so relaxed. We spent a good hour just floating around, I was tempted to close my eyes and go to sleep, but I knew if I did, Dennis would probably dunk me. So I just laid back and tried to image if this feeling of weightlessness is how it would feel walking in outer space.

As we walked back toward the shore, and the beach of bugs, Dennis said, "You have to wash really well, especially your hair, because the salt will turn your scalp into a consistency of peanut butter." If that wasn't enough motivation, I'm not sure what would be. After we showered, we walked up to the restaurant and had dinner. It was more or less a hamburger stand, but the food tasted good. After we ate, we walked one of the trails that led to the island's grasslands, and from a viewpoint, we could see in the distance a few dozen buffalo grazing, as well as several dozen antelope. On the way back to our campsite, Dennis said, "I think it's time to catch the bus home, my knee is hurting a little, and Austin is probably worried we won't make it back in time before work restarts."

I said, "It sounds great to me. I've had a great time and I'm ready to go home."

Back at our campsite, I decided to ask a question I had thought about asking several times but had chickened out before because I didn't have the nerve. Finally, I asked, "What was the Vietnam War really like?"

Dennis's jaw tightened. He took a deep breath and his nostrils flared as his chest rose and fell. He looked at me and said, "It was very scary, sometimes it felt like every nerve in my body was going to explode, and other times, I felt numb like you could stab me with a knife and I wouldn't feel it. It changed me, I feel guilty even today for some of the things I did, and yet I made a great friend and enjoyed myself, if that makes any sense."

"From the moment I left for boot camp, I was homesick, and I never really adjusted to the loneliness. Then going home on leave that Christmas made it worse because my heart was breaking and I didn' t feel I could tell anyone. I didn't want them to see me as a coward. When we reached Vietnam, I was so frightened by the stories I was hearing. We did a week of orientation and then they gave us our assignments. But before we were to be shuttled to new platoons, they gave us a twenty-four-hour furlough and bused us to Saigon. Our second lieutenant, said, 'Go out and get drunk, party with the girls, have fun, live life like you only get one chance, because tomorrow the only thing between you and death will be your gun, your training, and the grace of God. If that doesn't make you want to pee your pants, I don't know what does.'"

"After settling in with my platoon, life went through cycles of action and boredom, we would go on patrol, followed by days of doing mind-numbing tasks. That's when I started volunteering for cooking duty. It gave the day at least a routine."

I asked, "Did you ever have to kill someone?"

"I never had hand-to-hand combat with anyone," Dennis said. "But I fired my gun in several skirmishes, whether any of those rounds injured or killed someone, I don't know."

"Did you ever witness anyone die?" I asked.

Dennis very quietly answered, "Yes, and a good friend of mine lost his legs when he stepped on a land mine. He was only about twenty feet in front of me when it happened. Most of those events were very surreal, like everything happening is in slow motion until you wake up as from a nightmare."

"I still have nights when I can't get certain events out of my mind, but that doesn't happen as often as it did when I first returned."

"Probably the most profound effects on my life from the war are my drug and alcohol use. In Vietnam, drugs were everywhere. We smoked pot regularly, often in front of our commanding officers who were smoking it themselves. They didn't care, or at least they turned a blind eye to its use. We'd smoke to relax, and then we'd take speed to stay awake. Some of the guys in my unit never touched the stuff, while other guys were high the whole time they were there."

"I think I broke every one of the Ten Commandments more than once, during my time in Vietnam, and bad habits are hard to break."

I said, "I know I don't need to tell you this, but the Bible states if you break one of the Ten Commandments, you're guilty of them all, so I and everyone else are as guilty as you in God's eyes. Just remember God forgives us of our sins if we ask for forgiveness."

There was a brief pause between us. "I'm sorry you had to go through hell here on earth," I said, "but you can look forward to an eternity of peace in heaven.

"What makes me sad is there are millions of people who have lived their lives here on earth in peace, but will spend eternity in Hell, because they never accepted Jesus as their Savior. And what's really terrible is there's going be people who thought they would be going to Heaven when they die, only to find out God has rejected them because they rejected Jesus Christ as God's Son."

After our conversation, I think I understood Dennis much more than I ever did before.

As we watched the sun set over the Great Salt Lake, Dennis said, "What do you think is the greatest wonder of the world?"

"Are you talking about the Seven Wonders of the World?" I said.

"I know there are several lists. The wonders that come to mind are, the Great Pyramids of Giza, the Taj Mahal, the Great Wall of China, the Grand Canyon, the Eiffel Tower, the Leaning Tower of Pisa, and the Golden Gate Bridge."

I said, "I've now been across the Golden Gate Bridge, and it's a marvel of construction, but there are a lot of bridges. I've been to the Grand Canyon and it's nothing but a big hole in the ground. As far as beauty goes, the Columbia River Gorge is much prettier than the Grand Canyon, and I say it should be on the list. But my choice for the greatest wonder of the world has to be the Great Wall of China. I don't know if it is true or not, but I've heard it can be seen from the moon. The Great Wall is actually a series of walls over five thousand miles long built during the Ming Dynasty, a task that took an army of men nearly two thousand years to complete," I said.

"That's a good choice," Dennis said, "But I think there are others more deserving. The Seattle Space Needle, The Coliseum in Rome, Machu Picchu in Peru, Petra in Jordan, the Angkor Temple in Cambodia, the Statues of Easter Island, and Saint Basil's Cathedral in Russia. My personal favorites are Petra and Saint Basil's Cathedral. Ivan the Terrible commissioned an architect to design a church that would be unmatched in beauty to commemorate his victories in recent wars. When it was finished, he had his guards blind the man who designed it so he could not create another comparable building.

"But my choice for the greatest wonder of the world is Petra. It was unknown to the world outside of Jordan until 1812, when a Swiss archeologist discovered the red sandstone city with the edifices of its buildings carved into the hillsides. While it has several major buildings, its most famous building is the Treasury Building with its Greek columns and a magnificent carved façade. I don't think any other place on earth can match its grandeur and spectacular beauty."

"I've seen pictures of Petra," I said, "And it is amazing, but I still think the Great Wall of China is the greatest wonder."

"I have to disagree," Dennis said, "So this time, I guess we have a tie." My head was itching and when I scratched it; my scalp was soft and looked like peanut butter. Dennis said, "I told you so," as I headed off to the restroom to wash my hair again. After three washings, my scalp was raw, but clean.

In the morning, we packed our things, and headed back into Salt Lake City to find the Greyhound Bus Station. We were able to book seats on a bus leaving at 10:00 a.m. headed to Boise, with a stop in Twin Falls, Idaho. In Boise, we traded buses for a bus headed to Portland, with stops in

La Grande and Pendleton, Oregon. Our last bus would take us from Portland to Longview, Washington. Our total estimated time of travel sixteen hours. After booking our ride, we headed to get something to eat and make phone calls. I called my parents to let them know I should be home early tomorrow morning; we were in Salt Lake City and taking a Greyhound bus home. My mom said they couldn't wait to have me home again.

Since it was our last breakfast, and I had used my money sparingly, I decided to splurge and order something other than pancakes. I had a Denver Omelet, hash browns, a side order of bacon, and orange juice to drink. As we left the restaurant, I picked up a couple of postcards with a picture of the Great Salt Lake on the front. After breakfast, we made our way back to the bus station. Since we had a while to wait, we pulled out a deck of cards and played a game of hearts.

We boarded the bus along with thirty or so other riders. We found seats near the front of the bus and sat down across from a woman and her teenage daughter. As the bus pulled out and headed north, Dennis and I continued our card game. We exchanged three cards and then began. Dennis played the two of clubs and I played the ace of clubs. I then led out with the ace of diamonds, and Dennis followed suit with an eight. My strategy was to get rid of all my diamonds so that I could sluff-off the queen of spades, which Dennis had passed to me in our exchange of cards. But after playing the king and queen of diamonds Dennis still held the jack, so I played my last diamond the seven to which Dennis played his jack. Now in the lead, Dennis moved in for the kill and began playing spades, knowing I didn't have enough cards to protect the queen, and would eventually have to eat it. At the end of the hand, I held the queen of spades and three hearts for sixteen points while Dennis had ten hearts for ten points. Even though Dennis won the hand, I won the game as his ten points put him over the hundred-point total.

As I shuffled the cards to start another game, the young woman across from us asked if she could play. I looked at Dennis, and then said, "Sure, the more, the merrier." As she exchanged places with her mother, she introduced herself as Ann. She said they were on their way to Boise to see her grandfather who was in the hospital. Her father and two younger brothers had remained at home in Salt Lake City. As we began playing, she said, "Her Grandfather had suffered a stroke, but we were told he was going to be all right." As I looked around the bus, I began to wonder where were all these people going, and why, and did they all have a sad story like Ann's. Why had they taken the bus, were they poor, or sick, did they have only one family vehicle or no vehicle at all? I wondered if I would ever ride on a bus again in the future, and if so, why?

Ann was a good card player, and except for a hand where Dennis took every trick, giving us both twenty-six points, she won the game easily. I asked if she wanted to play The Greatest Game, and after explaining how it was played, she said, "Yes." To my surprise, Ann asked if she could pick the topic, Dennis said, "Go for it." Ann chose the greatest novel of all time. We drew cards for order of selection, and Dennis had the lowest card.

Dennis said, "The greatest novel of all time has to be either *To Kill a Mocking Bird* or *Gone With the Wind*. My choice is *Gone with the Wind*. It's the iconic American Novel. It's a love story set in the midst of the Civil War. They made it into a great movie; and everybody knows the famous line, "Frankly, Scarlet, I don't give a damn."

I had the second lowest card, so I went next, "My choice would be between *Moby Dick*, *Charlotte's Web*, and *Frankenstein*. Charlotte's Web by E.B. White has to be one of greatest novels written because every child has read it or had it read to them. *Moby Dick* usually comes up when people discuss great novels, but I didn't like it. Therefore, I choose *Frankenstein* by Mary Shelly. It's got a macabre background, a crazy scientist, and a monster. It's dark and sinister, it's a thriller that has entertained generations, and isn't that what a great novel should do?"

Ann said, "Each of your choices are good, but not as good as mine. There is only one clear choice for the greatest novel of all time, and it is the most widely read novel of all time *A Tale of Two Cities* by Dickenson. When you compare it to *War and Peace* which would be my second choice, or to other novels, none matches it in copies sold." Dennis said, "That's because stupid English teachers make their students read it. I don't know why they think it's so important, it's not even very good, you'd think they could come up with something less boring."

"It's time to vote," I said, "And Ann, I wouldn't count on getting Dennis's vote. Is anyone going to change their vote?"

Dennis said, "No."

Ann said, "Maybe."

"Okay," I said.

"Everyone for *A Tale of Two Cities*, I count no votes."

"All for *Frankenstein*, one vote, mine."

"That means *Gone with the Wind* wins.

"Congratulations, Dennis," Ann said. "You chose a great novel."

I said, "I still think *Frankenstein* is the greatest novel, they've only made one movie about *Gone with the Wind*, but they've made several based upon the novel Frankenstein. The truth is," I continued, "I've never read *A Tale of Two Cities* or *Gone with the Wind*, but I have watched the movies. I did read *Frankenstein* in middle school, and I liked it. My high school English teacher assigned us to read Alex Huxley's *A Brave New World*, now that was stupid!" After finishing our game, we sat back and relaxed for the rest of the trip to Boise.

We had an hour before our bus left for Portland, so we made our way to a nearby McDonald's for a Big Mac. "I love McDonald's fries," I said. "I heard the owner of McDonald's owned a struggling fast-food business in Chicago until one day, a salesman showed him a new machine that cooked french fries, which he bought the rights to, and, boom! McDonalds was a hit."

Dennis said, "That's not quite the truth, the owner of the McDonald's corporation is Ray Kroc, but he wasn't the original owner of McDonald's. He was a salesperson selling a new multi-blender milkshake machine not a french-fry machine, and two of his customers were the McDonald brothers who owned a fast food restaurant in California. Kroc realized the potential of their business and negotiated the exclusive rights to sell McDonald's franchises. He opened the first McDonald franchise in Illinois, and within a few years, there were hundreds spread across the United States. Mr. Kroc made his fortune not by selling hamburgers but by buying and selling real estate. He would buy the land where a new McDonald's franchise was to be built, and then turn around and sell or lease it to the franchise owner. Within a few years, he bought out the McDonald Brothers and now is the majority stockholder of the corporation."

"Smart man," I said. "As my father always says location, location, location."

As we boarded the bus for the 430-mile trip to Portland, I was sad and happy. Sad this wonderful journey was nearly over, but happy to get back home to my family and my own bed. That's the thing about vacations, you can't wait to go, and before too long, you can't wait to get back home. I settled into my seat, reclined it as much as possible, and prepared for a long nap. I told Dennis I planned to sleep until our arrival in La Grande. Dennis must have had the same idea because before we reached the freeway, he appeared to be asleep.

As the bus exited the freeway and came to a stop, I awoke, I looked at Dennis and he said "Were in La Grande, Oregon, and while you were sleeping, we picked up an hour as we moved from the Mountain Time Zone to the Pacific Time Zone." I asked Dennis how long he slept. He said, "Probably ninety minutes, or about halfway." As we pulled into the local Greyhound station, the bus driver announced we would have a scheduled fifteen-minute stop for pickup and drop-off, just enough time to use the restroom and stretch your legs. When we re-boarded, we had some new company. A young man was sitting in the row across from us where Ann and her mother had previously been prior to their departure in Boise. I introduced myself and he said,

"I'm Dale, and I'm a student at Eastern Oregon University in La Grande, and I'm headed home to Portland."

I asked him what he was majoring in, and he said, "Education with a bachelor's degree in history."

Dennis sat up and took notice. Dennis asked him, "What part of history do you hope to teach?"

Dale replied, "I enjoy world history the most." Dale asked where we were headed.

Dennis explained, "For the last few weeks, we had been hitchhiking across the Western United States, but we are now headed home to Longview, Washington."

Dale's eyes lit up, he said, "My roommate last year was from Longview, he's a defensive back on the EOU football team and a graduate from R.A. Long High School."

Dennis said, "That's where I went to high school."

Dale and Dennis hit it off well, and were soon discussing early civilizations and which one was the greatest, the Greeks, the Romans, the Egyptians, or the Persians. I listened intently, intrigued by their knowledge and their interpretation of the contributions each civilization has made to our modern society. I guess what surprised me the most was how well-versed Dennis was. He had as much knowledge or more than Dale who would soon have a degree in history. After their discussion, Dennis suggested playing The Greatest Game with the topic being the greatest military leader of all time. I felt my odds of winning where slim and none against Dennis and Dale, but I knew about a couple of great military leaders from World War II. So as not to embarrass myself, I volunteered to go first.

"My choices," I said, "Would be between Dwight D. Eisenhower, Gen. MacArthur, and George Patton. Eisenhower was the Commander of the Allied Forces in Europe during WWII, and the architect of the Normandy invasion. He is given much of the credit for the defeat of Hitler's Germany. On the strength of his military record, Americans elected him President of the United States. Gen. MacArthur is credited with defeating the Japanese. He was a huge hero but lost much of that respect when President Truman relieved him of his duty during the Korean War. Some say the real military genius of WWII was Gen. George Patton, but his military successes were marred by his inability to get along with his superiors and the media. He was so well respected by the Germans, who considered him their greatest foe. The Allies used him as a decoy to hide the true invasion point of Europe, and it worked. And for that reason, I choose Gen. Patton, he might have rubbed others the wrong way, but he accomplished every military task he was ever given and won more major battles than any other Allied general."

Dennis said, "Dale, you're next."

"My choice," Dale said, "Is Hannibal, the Carthaginian general who marched his army, which included war elephants, across Southern Europe and over the Alps into Northern Italy. He then launched a surprise attack on Rome. Taking on the Roman Army, the most formidable fighting force of ancient times, he defeated them in battle after battle. Hannibal occupied much of Italy for fifteen years until Rome launched a counter attack against Carthage, forcing him to return home to defend his homeland. Military historians have called Hannibal the Father of Military Strategy. The Romans respected him so much they adopted many elements of his military tactics. In fact, the Roman general who finally defeated Hannibal, studied and used Hannibal's own tactics in their last and decisive battle."

"There have been many great military leaders though the ages that have made their mark by leading mighty armies," Dennis said, "Such as Alexander the Great and Julius Caesar. They are all known for their victories, but few military leaders are known as great because of their losses. I choose George Washington, the American Revolutionary war hero. He never won a decisive battle against the British, but instead employed the strategy of avoiding large confrontations that might lead to total defeat. Gen. Washington knew his army was no match for the British

Army, so he only engaged in small skirmishes; he also understood the British controlled the seas and could provide a continual supply of troops and resources. Therefore, the only chance of winning was to prolong the war until the cost of victory became more than the British were willing to pay. After seven years, the British decided winning wasn't worth it. George Washington had his victory, and America had its independence."

I said, "Cool, it's now time to vote."

"Who votes for George Patton?"

"Who votes for Hannibal?"

"Who votes for George Washington?"

It's unanimous. Dennis and George Washington win.

I still thought Patton was the greatest, but how can you argue against the Father of Our Nation?

When we pulled into Pendleton, Oregon, the bus driver announced we would have a thirty-minute break and suggested a few places to eat. Dennis, Dale, and I walked up the street to the Dairy Queen. After ordering our food, Dennis went off to use the payphone, Dale and I seated ourselves at a booth. I said, "I've never been to the Pendleton Round-Up, but my grandfather says they have a great rodeo here." Dale said, "It's one of the top rodeos each year in prize money and attendance. It's also the only professional rodeo held on a grass field."

"While Pendleton is known regionally for its rodeo," Dale said, "Do you know what it is known for worldwide?"

"I do," I said, "Wool blankets and shirts. I happen to have a wool Indian blanket made by the Pendleton Woolen Mills on my bed."

Dennis picked up our order after using the phone and brought it to our booth. He said, "The company and the union has reached a settlement. It looks like we will be going back to work soon."

As the bus pulled out of Pendleton and headed for Portland, Oregon, on Interstate 84, we passed through fields of crops and scrub brush in a semi-aired desert. It was dusk, the sun had set, and the sky was trying to hold on to its last bit of light as we passed through Umatilla, Oregon. Here, the highway began to parallel the Columbia River, which we would follow all the way home. My excitement grew as we passed through the familiar communities of the Dallas, Hood River, Cascade Locks, and Troutdale. When we pulled into Portland, it was 12:30 p.m., the bus from Portland to Longview, Washington was scheduled to leave at 1:00 p.m. If the bus left on time, we would be at Dennis's apartment in just over an hour. As we traveled north, most of the other passengers were sleeping. But both Dennis and I were both wide awake, yet we didn't speak, I could tell his mind was elsewhere. As the miles grew fewer to our destination, I started to think about the future. College was scheduled to start in a few weeks and, more than likely, I wouldn't be called back to work, even though the strike had officially ended. It would take a few days to get the plant back up to speed and with so little time before school began, I was sure the summer employees were through. That was okay with me. I had plenty to do before classes began, and more than ever, I wanted to spend the rest of the time I had left with my family.

As the bus's wheels stopped rolling at the Longview Greyhound Station, Dennis and I disembarked from the bus, grabbed our things and began walking the few blocks to Dennis's apartment. As we walked, I realized summer was over. It was as clear as the cloudless moonlit sky. Fall had arrived in the Pacific Northwest. I thanked Dennis for taking me with him on his vacation. I said, "I will always remember the people we met and places we visited, but mostly, I just enjoyed being with you."

Dennis said, "I agree. I would rank it as the best hitch-hiking trip I've ever made, and I've made a few."

"So what's next for you?" I asked.

He said, "I plan on checking in with work tomorrow and find out what's going on. Then I think I'll make an appointment with my doctor to have my knee looked at. It's been hurting for a while and the walking we did has made it worse. It might just be a buildup of fluid, or I might need surgery, I'll see."

"What about you?" Dennis said.

"After I sleep, I'm going to take a long, hot shower, then catch up on the family news. College starts in a few weeks, so I'm sure I'll have my hands full getting ready to move." As I put my things into my car I said, "If I don't see you before I leave, I'll see you at Thanksgiving."

It felt good to slip into my bed and lay my head on a soft pillow with the covers pulled up to my neck; it was good to be home. I had originally planned to sleep in, but as daylight streamed through my bedroom window, it seemed much more important to get up and have breakfast with my parents than to sleep for a few more hours. So I got up and made my way upstairs, they were sitting at the kitchen table, drinking their morning cup of coffee when I entered the room. Before I said anything, I walked over to them and gave each of them a hug. Then I sat down to share the details of my trip.

Just before I left for college, I got a postcard from Rosemary. She said, "Thanks for the encouragement." She said she was doing better and had started going to church.

− 13 −

The Years
between Summers Two
and Three

A S I UNPACKED my things in my dorm room, my roommate Lance arrived with his stuff. He was 6'2" and built like a brick house. As we introduced ourselves, I learned he was a linebacker on the college football team, he loved 1960s music, and liked to play poker. It was a good beginning; we talked for hours about sports and music.

Golf didn't start until spring semester, but for those competing for a spot on the team, we received our golf course pass as soon as school began. Our coach expected us to play as often as possible, with the minimum being eighteen holes three times a week. There were three returning golfers, and nine freshmen competing for seven team spots. Everyone knew the nine of us freshmen were competing for four spots. During the first week of college, I tried to set a schedule and get into a routine. My classes were over by 1:00 p.m., my goal was to be on the golf course each day by 2:00 p.m., and have my practice completed by 6:00 p.m., so I could get back to school, get something to eat, and be in the library to study by 7:00 p.m. To size up my chances of making the team, I tried to play with at least two other freshmen I would eventually be competing against each day. From what I could tell, my chances were favorable.

On Saturdays, when there was a home football game, most of the guys from our dorm sat together in the student section to cheer on our team and Lance. Being a freshman, Lance played only on the kickoff team, so the more points the team scored, the more opportunities Lance got to show off his skills. At the last home game of the season, the members of our hall started chanting, "We want Lance, we want Lance." The coach didn't play him, but it did make Lance feel appreciated.

By the time, Thanksgiving rolled around the weather had turned cold and wet, and the days I could practice were limited. Lance got mononucleosis and left school and returned home. So I had the room to myself. For Thanksgiving break, I packed only a few things to take home, mostly clothes that needed to be washed.

As usual, we had a huge family Thanksgiving dinner, which included extended family members. I had a lot to share about college and golf and news to catch up on from others. Dennis was there, and I wanted him to know that because of our summer trip, I had decided to major in history. We didn't see each other that Christmas.

As winter turned to spring and golf got underway, the question of who would make the golf team had become much clearer. After a series of challenges, three of us were battling for two spots. After shooting a two over par 74 in the first competition, I secured a place on the seven-member team.

The season was tough; we traveled all across the Pacific Northwest and to Northern California to play our competition. The comradeship I enjoyed on my high school team was nonexistent. While we played for the same college, my teammates were also my competition, and to be feared as much as the players from other schools. That being said, the team and I had a successful season. I played well and moved up to number-three man by the season's end, and would be the top player returning for next year's team.

I enjoyed my first year of college. I found myself falling more in love with history with each class I took, I established some good friendships, and I couldn't wait for next year's golf season.

Upon returning home for the summer, I immediately began looking for a job. The economy had taken a small dip and the job I anticipated on having at the boat factory disappeared. No one was buying yachts. However, Austin and Dennis told me of a friend they had who owned a lumberyard that needed someone for the summer. I called the owner, and he had me come in for an interview. He hired me, and I started work the next day. As part of my job, I mixed paint, delivered lumber, operated the fork-lift, stocked shelves, helped customers, and worked as a cashier.

In late June, Jack and Renee showed up on their honey-moon. Dennis and I had dinner with them, and they filled us in on the latest news—Willow had taken a fall and bro-ken a hip, but she was back at home now and doing fine. The doctors gave her instructions to stay off her feet, but she refused to listen. Instead, she spent hours arranging the flowers and decorating the church for their wedding, and had to come to the wedding in a wheelchair the next day. Kit is doing well, and Casey is in remission, but the doctors are unsure for how long it will last. They stayed the night at Dennis's place before heading on north to Victoria, British Columbia, a favorite place of honeymooners.

Several of my friends from high school had formed a slow pitch softball team and they asked me to play. We played twice a week, on Tuesdays and Thursdays. One day, in early August, I was the only employee at the lumberyard when a semi-truck loaded with pallets of sacked cement showed up. I sprinted out to start up the forklift, but it wouldn't start. The truck driver became irate and kept cursing and swearing. After fifteen minutes, I told him I couldn't get the forklift started, and I didn't know how to fix it. After more swearing and cussing, he told me to start unloading it by hand, he wasn't coming back this way, and he should have been on his way ten minutes ago. So I started unloading the four pallets that were ours. There were fifty bags to a pallet and each bag weighed eighty pounds. I unloaded the bags as fast as I could, and I got no help from the driver, who did nothing but sit in his truck and mutter. Twenty minutes later, I finished. My back hurt like crazy, and I could barely stand up straight, but at least I didn't have to listen to the foul-mouthed truck driver anymore.

When my shift finally ended, my back still hurt. I had lifted with my back and not my legs so many times in my hurry to unload the truck, I had definitely done some damage. Nevertheless, because it was a Thursday, which meant softball, I grabbed something to eat and headed for the softball fields. As I warmed up, I could feel pain in my left thigh and in my lower back, so I did a little extra stretching and figured I'd be okay. We played a double header that night. With each swing of the bat, I felt the pain in my back get worse. By the time the second game finished, I could hardly stand up straight, and there was pain in both my legs and in my back.

When I got home, I decided to use my parents' whirlpool bathtub to see if it would help with the pain. This was a poor decision. After thirty minutes in the tub, I couldn't get out, no matter what I tried, I could not lift myself up. To make matters worse, no one was home to help me. Finally, I heard someone come home. It turned out to be my father. I yelled for help, but it took several minutes to get him to respond. When he finally figured out I was serious, he came to my aid. Dad lifted me up out of the tub, gave me his robe to put on, and then more or less carried me to the living room where I laid back down on the floor. Dad got a hot pad and placed it on my back, and I remained there until the next morning.

When Mom woke me up for work, I couldn't move, and I began to panic. I had no mobility, and could barely roll from side to side. My parents got out an old stretcher they had, and I rolled on to it. With help, they placed me into the back of our station wagon and took me to the hospital. When we got there, a doctor examined me, and said I would need to get up so they could take x-rays. I told him, if I could get up, I would have walked in here instead of coming in on a stretcher. They put me in a cubicle and had a nurse massage my back for twenty minutes. Then the doctor with the help of two nurses helped me to my knees. After a few seconds, they lifted me to a semi-standing position, and I hobbled into the x-ray room. I stood there with my hands on my knees, shaking. When the doctor said, "I need you now to straighten up and stand tall." I mustered all my strength and forced myself to stand erect. The last thing I remember is saying, "Everything is getting dark!"

When I woke up, I was lying on a table, and a nurse was taking my pulse. The doctor said I'd been out for about fifteen minutes, but fainting had caused all my muscles to relax, and made it easier to put my back into place. He gave me some pain pills and ordered me to keep ice, not heat, on my back for the next seventy-two hours. I missed four days of work, and when I returned, my boss told me not to lift anything at all! I worked the rest of the summer as a cashier.

Upon returning to college, I concentrated on my studies and the weekly physical therapy sessions I had for my back injury, foregoing fall golf practices. My favorite class was Ancient Civilizations, the lectures were full of interesting stories, and I spent all my extra time reading the books on the assigned reading list. I even changed my TV viewing habits as a result, I read for an hour each night before going to bed except on Mondays. On Mondays, I watched Monday Night Football, and after the game, I'd visit with my father on the phone.

During my first year at college, I realized the TV station I watched Monday Night Football on aired the game an hour earlier than the TV station at home. So I'd call home each Monday night before the game had started on his station, and we'd bet a milkshake on who'd win the game. I won so many milkshakes during my first two years of college, Dad didn't want to bet anymore. Of course, I never shared my secret. I love chocolate milkshakes.

Another interesting event happened during my sophomore year, toward the end of the college basketball season. I was sitting with an acquaintance and a few of his friends. At each home basketball game, if you bought a program you had a chance to win a new car. The promotion was sponsored by a local car dealership, and at halftime, they would draw a number, and if it corresponded with the number in your program, you could attempt to make five free throws in row, and if you did, you won a new car.

My acquaintance purchased two programs before the game started, and at halftime, when they read the winning number, his was one number off. I heard one of his friends say, "Don't worry about it, you'll get it next time."

I looked at his friend, and asked, "How can you be sure of that?" My acquaintance told his friend to shut up, but it was already too late. His friend explained that before the start of each game, the people who ran the promotion chose five programs, wrote their numbers down, and then sold the programs. Over the loud complaint of my acquaintance, he said, "We know the person who sells those specific programs, and he sells two of the five to us at each home game."

At the next home game, I sat with three other friends. As the announcer began, his sales pitch about winning a new car, I told them, "See that guy," and pointed out where he was sitting. "The announcer is going to call out the winning number, it's going to be his, he'll go to the free throw line, make five free throws in a row, and win the car." My friends looked at me as if I must be high on drugs, but when they called out his number, and he went to the free throw line and made five in a row, they thought I must be clairvoyant!

They were all staring at me and asking, "How did you know that?" I told them I knew him and he was an awesome high school basketball player. He played two years of community college basketball and then transferred here. He tried out for the university team but didn't make the cut, and now he spends all his spare time shooting free throws. When I shared the rest of the story, all they could say was unbelievable, unbelievable! A few weeks later, I opened the college newspaper, and the headline read, "Three students expelled for inappropriate behavior," sure enough, it was my acquaintance and his friends. The article also reported the winner would not receive the car, and the cancellation of all future promotions.

That spring, I made the golf team as the number-three man, but I struggled being consistent, and I felt pain in my back increasingly. Halfway through the season, I was demoted to playing sixth man. The coaches and I met and we decided it would be in my best interest to take a break and see if I could get my back to heal and try to play again next year. I felt crushed; this was my dream. But I vowed to myself to come back stronger and better than I had ever been next year.

The happiest moment of my sophomore year came when I declared my major as history, and took the placement test to enter the College of Education. I finally felt like I knew what I wanted to be. If golf didn't work out, I was going to be a high school history teacher.

During the summer of 1976, Austin organized a weekend trip to Seattle to watch the Oakridge Boys in concert on Friday night, and the Seattle Mariners play the Yankees on Saturday. Austin, Dennis, myself, and three other young men from church crowded into Austin's van and we headed north Friday afternoon. The plan included staying at another relative's house for the night. The Oakridge Boys at the time were still a gospel group and had not made their change to more mainstream country music. At the concert, Dennis told me he was thinking of moving to Sonoma, California. Shelia had found a small restaurant for sale that had connections to several Napa Valley wineries, and she wanted him to join her to run the place as a partner. I said, "Shelia from San Francisco? How long has this been going on?"

He said, "Over the last two years. We've met a couple of times in San Francisco, and she came up to Washington last month."

I said, "So is this serious." Dennis smiled but didn't give an answer. The Yankees beat the Mariners 7-1. We all had a great weekend, but Dennis had the best. In September, Dennis moved to Sonoma, California. The paths of our lives were once again diverging.

I worked hard during the fall of 1976 on my golf game, and I exercised to strengthen my back all winter, but three weeks into golf season, my back problems returned. Even before that, I knew deep down in my heart, I was never going to be a professional golfer. My father always said, "Following dreams can be tricky, sometimes you reach your goal, other times you realize what you thought you wanted wasn't what you really wanted at all." What I realized was I loved the game of golf, but I wanted to be a teacher even more.

I graduated cum laude in 1978 with a major in history and a minor in coaching. I applied for a half dozen teaching jobs within driving distance from home, but I was unable to secure a position. So I signed up to substitute at the local high schools. For the first half of the school year,

I worked nearly every day, but rarely in the same classroom. In December, the principal at Woodland said there was a job opening for me at Clark College in the High School Continuation Program if I wanted it. He had already spoken to them about me, and all I had to do was call and tell them I wanted the job, which I did. Starting in January, I had my own classroom, where I taught Washington State history. It was about this same time I met my future wife. A good friend of mine invited me to come to his church one Sunday where I met this beautiful blue-eyed girl with long hair and a smile that could light up the world.

I applied for teaching jobs again during the spring of 1979, and I was hired by a small school in Eastern Washington to teach and coach. As soon as I had a job, I proposed, and she said yes. Dennis didn't make it to the wedding, but we did receive a nice gift, and the card was signed from Shelia and Dennis.

When I reported to my new school to start work, they informed me that they hadn't hired a girl's volleyball coach, and I was now the new coach. On the first day of practice, I introduced myself and explained I had played volleyball and loved the game, but I had never coached the sport. I told them if they would teach me the skills and practice drills, I'd teach them how to win. On the second day of practice, a young freshman girl came up to me and said her grandmother wanted to meet me. She then escorted me over to the bleachers where her grandmother was sitting. I smiled and asked how I could help her.

She said, "My granddaughter tells me you're her new teacher and coach, and this is your first teaching position. Where did you go to grade school at?"

I said, "Woodland Elementary School."

She said, "My name is Mrs. Zule, and my first teaching position was at Woodland Elementary School. I had a curly–haired, blue-eyed boy in my second grade class with your name, would that be you?" I couldn't believe it, I'd move clear across the state to a little town in the middle of nowhere, and to my surprise, who should I meet, my second grade teacher. What a small world. I grew up in Woodland and wound up teaching in Northport. She grew up in Northport and wound up teaching for years in Woodland. Since that day, my wife always jokes, "I can't take you anywhere without you running into someone you know."

At Clark College, I had taught just Washington State history, but in my new school, I taught World history, US history, Washington State history, Contemporary World Problems, and a PE class. All this, plus I coached volleyball, basketball, and baseball. As I look back now, I realize it might have been hard then, but it made me a good teacher. One of the best lessons I have ever learned came during that first year at Northport.

After losing two out of four non-league volleyball matches, we began to win. The girls had won fifteen straight matches, they had taught me the practice drills, and I'd kept my word and taught them how to compete. But when we lost our last match of the season, I was disappointed. When the match was finished, the girls could see I was upset, they had played terribly. They had made too many service errors and misplayed too many bumps and sets.

When I confronted the team about these issues, I said, "What happened out there tonight, it looked like you had forgotten everything we've worked on all season."

The team captain looked at me and said, "It was your fault we lost."

"My fault," I said, "I didn't serve the ball out of bounds half the time, or spike the ball into the net over and over again."

She said, "No, but once we made a few mistakes, you started yelling at us, you never did that before, and that just made us more nervous, and then we made more mistakes, and you yelled even louder."

I learned two things that night. One: girls are not boys, and second: screaming and yelling is not coaching. It's just screaming and yelling whether you're coaching girls or boys. The same thing applies to teaching; encouragement always wins out over criticism. I had been coached by coaches who yelled my whole life, even when we were winning. On that night, I learned a lesson. They taught me how to coach.

In the next fifteen years, my teaching career took me to three different schools where I taught and coached. I earned a master's degree and our family grew by two as my wife gave birth to two sons, Matt and John. The occasions of which I had time to spend with Dennis during this period was limited to a few holidays and funerals.

– 14 –

The Third Summer

I REMEMBER IT was a Saturday morning in late May, 1993, when the phone rang. My wife answered it, and said, "It's your father." I picked up the extension and said, "Hello, Dad, I was just thinking about calling you."

He said, "I've got some bad news. Dennis is in the hospital and the doctors says he only has three, maybe four months to live. He has an advanced case of sorosis of the liver, and other medical complications. They've stabilized him, and they're going to move him to a local nursing home in a few days."

I asked, "When did all this come about? Last thing I heard, he was in California."

Dad said, "Apparently, he hasn't felt well for a while. He sold his interest in the restaurant to his partner about three months ago, but never said anything about being in poor health to anyone. Then last week, he showed up at his parents' house. The next day, they took him to the VA hospital."

I said, "School will be out for the summer in a couple of weeks, we were planning to come home for a visit before we take the boys to Disneyland, so we will see everyone then. Please let Dennis know he's in our prayers."

I shared the news with my wife after getting off the phone. That afternoon, we went into town, and picked up a card and ordered some flowers delivered. As we drove back home, I confided I was scared about Dennis dying as much as I was sure he felt scared. I asked her what I should write on the card, "I'm at a loss for words."

"Just tell him you love him and why," she said. I spent the rest of the day alone in our bedroom putting my thoughts together.

> Dear Dennis,
>
> I wish the purpose of this card was to wish you a Happy Birthday rather than to share my deep felt sorrow about your illness. But in a way it is a Happy Birthday Card, we both know life here on earth is like a blink of an eye compared to eternity, and those of us who have placed our faith in Jesus Christ will spend forevermore with our Savior in heaven. I know your days here on earth are short, but I pray you will soon have a new body that will never die.

School will be out in a few weeks and we plan to come over and spend time visiting.

Love Nathan & Family

There were only two days left of school, and the kids were all excited about going to Grandpa and Grandma's and the start of summer vacation. I was sitting in my fake leather lazy-boy chair, correcting papers, and half watching TV when the phone rang. I said, "Hello."

The voice on the other end said, "Hello, son."

I said, "Hi, Mom."

She said, "We just got a phone call, and apparently Dennis took a turn for the worse last night and passed away early this morning. Your father is taking it hard, but he wanted you to know. They are planning the funeral now, and it will be on Saturday to allow for those who will need time to travel."

About all I could say was, "Thank you for calling. I love you. Tell Dad I love him. We'll see you in few days." I hung up the phone as the tears streamed down my face.

I put the phone down, kicked back in my chair, and covered my face with my hands. The time frame was all wrong, in a few days, I would have been there to visit with him before he died. I kept kicking myself for not going home before now, then clear as day, I could see Dennis's face, and he said, "It's okay, I'm in a better place now."

School got out on Wednesday and Dennis's funeral was Saturday. Thursday night, we packed our dress clothes for the funeral and enough other clothes for our vacation. Friday morning, we left early for the five-hour drive home. On the way, I decided to introduce my family to The Greatest Game, we had been on long family trips before, but we had never played the game. It just seemed right to play it now. After explaining how to play the game, I said we'd play four rounds so each of us of could make a selection.

"I'll go first," I said. Trying to make a selection we could all understand and relate to, I chose the greatest Mariner baseball player of all time. I said, "My choice is Harold Reynolds, the best second baseman the Mariners have ever had. He's been chosen twice as an all-star, and one season, he stole sixty bases. Okay, sweetheart, your turn."

"I choose Randy Johnson, the Big Unit. He's the best pitcher in baseball as well as the greatest Mariner. The Mariners win every time he pitches."

I said, "Not every time."

"Well it seems like that to me," she said.

Matt said, "Dad, do you remember the video of the time? One of Randy's pitches hit a bird and killed it. The bird flew right in front of the plate when he was pitching and he hit it!"

I said, "I do, but in this game, you don't want to help someone else, Matt."

"John, it's your turn."

"I choose Edgar Martinez. Ken Griffey Jr. is fantastic, and Jay Burhner is awesome, but Edgar's my favorite player. If he isn't the greatest now, he will be soon. He's the best clutch player I've ever seen."

"Matt, what's your choice?" I said.

"Well I think you guys are trying to make it easy for me because I'm the youngest, because everyone knows the greatest player the Mariners have ever had or will have, except for maybe for Alex Rodriguez, is Ken Griffey Junior. He hits more home runs than anyone else. He's the best center fielder in baseball, and he's going to break Babe Ruth's home run record."

"It's time to vote," I said. "How many votes for Harold."

"How many for Randy Johnson."

"How many for Edgar!"

"How many for Junior."

"We have a tie, the boys both win!"

Matt said, "You did that on purpose, Dad."

"Your turn to go first, sweetheart," I said.

"I choose as my topic the greatest flower and my choice is the carnation. The carnation is the flower of love. Light-red carnations represent admiration, while dark-red carnations denote deep love and affection. White carnations represent pure love and good luck. Pink carnations have the most symbolic significance. According to a Christian

legend, carnations first appeared on earth when Jesus died.
The Virgin Mary shed tears at Jesus's plight, and carnations sprang up from where her tears fell. Thus, the pink
carnation has become the symbol of a mother's undy-
ing love."

"Your turn, Matt," I said.

"I think the greatest flower is the sunflower because you
can eat its seeds, and it must be the tallest of all flowers."

"Is that it?" I asked.

"That's it," he said.

"Okay, John, it's your turn."

"I believe the greatest flower is the lily. I like them
because they smell good, they come in lots of colors, and
Grandma has a whole bunch of them around her house.
She even has night lily's that close up at night and go to
sleep and wake up again in the morning."

"My choice is the tulip for the greatest flower," I said.
"Most people think tulips originated in Holland, but the
truth is they were first cultivated in modern-day Turkey
during the Ottoman Empire. However, most of the varie-
ties are the results of growers from the Netherlands. When
the first tulip bulbs arrived in Europe, people went crazy.
The King of France once paid in today's money a million
dollars for the first bulbs of a new variety. Tulip bulbs were
worth more than gold at one time in Holland, and people
bought and sold stock in tulips just like people in America

trade on the New York stock exchange. It was the flower of the rich and nobility, but like the stock market crash of 1929, the tulip boom went bust because of over production. It is my favorite because of their vivid color and their beautiful shape."

"It's time to vote," I said. "The choices are the carnation, sunflower, lily, and tulip. How many for the carnation." As I looked there were three hands in the air. With three votes, Mom wins.

"You're next, Matt, what's your selection?"

"Dad, can we quit," he said. "I'm tired."

"Me too," John said.

When we finally arrived Friday afternoon, the kids could hardly contain themselves as they piled out of the car. They said their greetings to their grandparents and then rushed to the garage to grab their fishing poles and headed for the river. After being in the car for five hours, I didn't feel like more sitting either, so Dad and I decided to follow the boys down to the river and watch them fish for a while. As we walked, Dad shared he, Austin, and Austin's father had spent several evenings with Dennis in the last few weeks, and he felt Dennis was now with God in heaven. He said, "Next to you, he was always my favorite little man."

After several hours, the boys returned from fishing. John was tired and he fell asleep on the couch in the living room. When he woke up, he started crying because he thought he'd missed breakfast. Breakfast has always been a favorite part of the trip to Grandma's because she serves French toast with peanut butter and hot maple syrup. Once we convinced John he hadn't missed breakfast, he stopped crying and calmed down.

The next morning, we headed to the funeral. It was a traditional family and friends gathering to say good-bye to a loved one. There were more people there than I thought there would be. There were people from church who had not seen Dennis for years, relatives you only see at funerals, men from the boat factory, and dozens of others I didn't know. There were three faces there I wasn't surprised to see. I guess I somehow just expected them to be there, though I had no basis for my feelings. Standing in the back of the funeral hall as I entered I saw Shelia and Rosemary. As soon as they saw me, they came over to greet me. They had a man with them. I gave them both a hug, then Rosemary introduced the man as her husband, and then she whispered to me, "I met him at church." The other face I hadn't seen in years, but I recognized him immediately, Joe Santino. Dennis remembered Joe from our trip to San Francisco, and when Shelia and he opened their restaurant in Sonoma, he contacted Joe to supply them with seafood.

After the funeral and the burial service, everyone went to the church for a potluck. I invited Rosemary, her husband, and Shelia to join my wife and others at our table.

Rosemary showed us pictures of their three children, and Shelia told us she had decided to sell the restaurant and move back to Los Angeles. "It just wasn't fun anymore without Dennis," she said. I knew their relationship went much deeper than just business partners, and the loss to her was greater than anyone other than Rosemary and I knew, but she never shared those things with me.

After dinner, most everyone made their way to the sanctuary of the church for the tradition of sharing memories about the deceased. After several others had gone, I stood up to share. I said, "I don't know if everyone knows, but Dennis was quite the historian. One summer, Dennis and I made a trip to San Francisco, and all along the way, he regaled me and others about local and ancient history. In fact, his love of history rubbed off on me, and that's why I became a history teacher. Once, Dennis said to me, 'Have you ever wished you could go back in time, change what you've done, and start your life from that point again?' I can honestly say, as far as the time we spent together, and the memories I have of those days, I wouldn't change them for anything."

When the gathering at the church finished and everyone was saying good-bye to each other, Aunt Sarah, Dennis's mom came up and hugged me, and said, "Thank you for what you said." She then handed me an envelope and said, "Dennis wanted you to have this."

As we drove back home, I clutched the envelope tightly, my wife asked if I was going to open it. I said, "Later." When we got home, I said, "I'm going to take a walk, and I'll be back in a little bit." I decided to head down to the river. I found an old stump and sat down and wept. I guess I just needed to emotionally unwind. I took the envelope out my pocket and opened it up. In it I found a letter and a second envelope. I began reading the letter:

Dear Nathan,

You've always been a good friend and someone I could trust. I have one last request, will you please mail this letter for me, when you look at the address I know you will recognize the address. Relationships have never been my strong suit, I have always hurt the people I loved the most. In the envelope is a letter and a check for most of the proceeds from my share of the restaurant, please make sure she gets it.

When I was young, I accepted Jesus as my savior, but as a teenager, I thought the world had far more to offer so I rebelled against God, and choose to live like my worldly friends. Now as my life nears its end, I can't help but thinking about the story of the "Prodigal Son" who after years of sinful living returns home to find his father willing to welcome him back. When the Prodigal Son returns, his brother, the faithful son, is jealous about his father's lavish treatment of his returning brother. When the father recognizes his faithful son is unhappy, he asks him why. The faithful son replies it's not fair the way you are treating him, do you not remember how he broke your heart, and now after squandering all the inheritance you gave him, he returns for more. To which the father replies, "He is my son as you are, I loved him before he left, I loved him while he was gone, and I will continue to love him, my son was lost but now is found. Neither he, nor I, or you, can change the past, but we can enjoy the future."

I wasted the relationship I should have had with my earthly father, and more importantly, the relationship with my heavenly father, and for that, I am truly sorry. But, I look forward to enjoying the future with both.

Love, Dennis

I placed my return address on it and mailed the letter the next day.

$$- 15 -$$

W E STAYED WITH my parents for a few more days
before departing for the vacation we had promised
the boys to Disneyland. After several days at the
Southern California theme park, it was time to head home.
Instead of returning by the direct route, we cut across to the
coast and stopped in San Francisco. We visited Fisherman's
Wharf, Golden Gate Park, and the Japanese Tea Garden,
and I told them about the summer I hitchhiked here
with Dennis.

Later, we visited the Redwood Forest, and we walked
around the base of the same trees Dennis and I walked
around nearly twenty years before. We stayed a few more
days in Woodland at my parents' house before returning
home. On the final leg of our journey home, I made a
short detour to a music store to purchase a few CDs. I had
decided to revive my love for the great songs of the Beach
Boys. I bought their albums "All Summer Long," "Summer
Days," and "Endless Summer."

After our extended stay away, the yard needed mowing badly, plus, the usual list of summer maintenance on the house needed to be completed. However, listening to the Beach Boys made the time go by quickly. It reminded me of working with Dennis on the rock crusher when I was nine. When the necessary projects were done, I settled into my summer routine of playing a couple of rounds of golf a week, some lake fishing with the boys, and listening to music.

Early in August, we traveled to Seattle for a two-night stay, we watched the Mariners play the Yankees twice. The Yankees won both games, Dennis would have been happy. In mid-August, the boys went to Bible Camp for a week. Six days without kids, alone with my wife, it was like being newlyweds for one week.

One day, in late August, the doorbell rang around 11:00 a.m. As I made my way from the back of the house, I was thinking it must be a delivery from UPS. However, when I opened the door, there stood a young woman dressed in pink shorts and sandals, wearing sunglasses. She said, "You might not remember me." She took off the glasses. "But years ago, you read me this book." She held it in her hand. "I'm Casey."

I looked at the book, looked at her, and all I could say was, "Yes, yes, I remember, you look just like your mother."

By that time, my wife had arrived at the door, and she was looking at me somewhat quizzical. I invited Casey in as I explained to my wife who she was. Once we sat down, I couldn't help but ask about her health. She said, "I'm fine now." And smiled. Her smile reminded me of Dennis's.

"You're probably wondering why I am here," she said. "A lot has changed in my life in the last few weeks, and I was hoping you could help me to understand some things. Let me start from the beginning. A few weeks ago, my grandmother received the letter you sent her. She gave it to my mother. She called me, crying, and asked me to come over to her house, I asked her what was wrong, and she said she'd explain when I got there. I hadn't heard her cry so much since I was little and the doctors told her I had leukemia. When she finally stopped sobbing, she said someone very dear to her had died. I said who. She said, 'Your father.'

"I gasped. I didn't know what to say or how to react. She had never shared his name with me, and now he had died, and I'd never know him. She had always said she found out she was pregnant after their relationship was over and that their lives were moving in two different directions, so she never told him. I trusted her, and never questioned her story. Now she's telling me something different. She began crying again, and then I started crying, and then she hugged me and we just held each other for a long time.

"Then she told me I had met my father once, but they had both agreed it was in my best interest for it not to be revealed. I was sick and more than likely going to die and I didn't need the added stress. She then reminded me of that summer and the two men who visited us. You read me *The Star Tree*, and later we went swimming out at the lake."

I said, "I remember."

"A few weeks later, I had an operation where the doctors injected me with bone marrow from a donor. The leukemia went into remission, and I got better. Eventually, the doctors proclaimed me officially cured. It turns out the donor was my father."

"I didn't know that," I said.

"I do remember your father saying his knee was hurting not too long after we left your place, so we took a Greyhound bus home, and he took a few days off to have knee surgery when we returned. It appears now the truth is he wanted to get home quickly so the doctors could remove some of his bone marrow for you."

"I guess I just want to understand why he would save my life and then never come to see me again. Why would he give me all this money?"

I said, "Casey, I'm not sure I can answer that for you, but I will tell you what I know, and I'd be happy to tell you a few things about your father. I can tell you he loved you and your mother. He never told me that in so many words, but I could see it in the way he looked at the two of you during the time we spent with you. I was as much in the dark then as you are now, but Dennis said things I didn't understand then. I do now.

"The first thing I noticed was while I was reading to you your book. Your mom and Dennis were talking secretly, and when they rejoined us, they both had been crying, which meant what they were talking about was emotional for both of them. Later, when we were at the lake, Dennis said to me, 'You know, for a few weeks, several years ago, I actually laid here staring out at this lake. I forgot about the war and believed joy was possible.' In my heart, I knew he was talking about his love for your mother. A few minutes later, he said, 'Have you ever wished you could go back in time and change what you've done, and start your life again from that point?' I think he was talking about your mom and you, I think he wished he had the both of you in his life, and if he could go back in time, he'd change it so you were a family. Before we left to go home that summer, your mother and father took a long walk together, whatever they discussed, I'm sure they thought they were making good decisions, based upon what they thought was best for you. Even if it meant Dennis would not be a part of your life.

"I think your mom told you the truth when she said their lives were going in two different directions. Your mom had her plans to go college and become a teacher, while Dennis didn't seem to have any definite plans. He lived his life that way, never wanting to be responsible for anyone else. I think your mom sensed that. Don't get me wrong, your father was a great guy and fun to be around. He was just a free spirit.

"Do you remember what you told me the day we met? You said, you would be okay. God would take care of you. I think God did take care of you. Dennis and I had no plans to hitchhike to San Francisco until the strike happened. If that hadn't happened, we never would have hitchhiked that summer or probably any other summer. If the strike hadn't lasted as long as it did, we would have never continued from San Francisco to Loveland, and if we had never come to Loveland that summer, your father would have never known you were sick or that he could make you well again.

"Why he never came to see you again, I don't know. Maybe he didn't feel he deserved to be a part of your life, or he wanted to respect your mother's wishes, maybe he was just afraid. Why he gave you his money? Maybe he was trying to right a wrong, and since you're his only legacy, he thought you should have it. One thing I'm positive of is he did not want this money to drive a wedge between you and your mother. He wanted only the best for the both of you. I'm not sure he thought your mom would even share with you where it came from.

"I don't know everything about your father, but these things I do know. Dennis loved to cook. He spent most of his life working as a chef. When I was little, he used to make my sisters and me peanut butter, chocolate chip, and coconut pancakes.

"Your father was a boy of summer. He loved baseball, and his favorite team was the New York Yankees. He loved music, especially the Beach Boys, and the Beatles. He loved to hitchhike. I think he was happiest when he was traveling and seeing new places or revisiting old ones. He loved the California sun, and more than any other city, San Francisco. He was a history buff. He was extremely knowledgeable about Pacific Northwest history and ancient world history. I learned as much from listening to him as I did in most of my history classes in college. He was a happy-go-lucky person, but he spent most of his life by himself. He was married once, but they got divorced. He told me they realized they didn't really love each other once they stopped partying, and the only thing they had in common was drugs and alcohol. In the end, alcohol would be his demise.

"We use to play a game called The Greatest Game in which you chose a topic, then each player gives his or her opinion, and then you debate who is right. What your father taught me was that the greatest game is life. Don't waste it, see and do as much as you can. More importantly, love those who God gives you to love."

When I finished, I looked at Casey, trying to read her face for some type of clue if what I had told her was what she was looking for, but all I saw was Dennis. After a few seconds, she said, "Thank you, that helps. I guess what I really wanted was to make a connection with someone who really knew him. Maybe get a few pictures of him."

"I don't think I have any pictures of Dennis, but I know someone who does, and I think she would like very much to meet you. It's a little bit of a drive, but I know it will be worth it."

We invited Casey to stay the night at our house and she accepted. That evening, I remembered the postcards I had purchased when Dennis and I had stayed at the Great Salt Lake, and after a few minutes of rummaging, I found them. I offered them to Casey. "It's not a picture, but they are from the trip we made to Loveland that summer." She graciously accepted them. The next morning, we drove to Longview.

As we entered the driveway and came to a stop, I saw the curtains in the window move. As we walked up the steps, the front door opened, and there stood my Aunt Sarah. There was a look of expectation on her face, and she was dressed in her Sunday best. I said, "Aunt Sarah, this is Casey, your granddaughter."

Aunt Sarah threw her arms around Casey and hugged her in a loving embrace, and then she seated us at a table set for a feast. It was as if Aunt Sarah and Casey already knew each other, and they were catching up on what had happened in each other's lives after a long separation. It was if Casey was the prodigal son returning home.

I see Casey now at least once a year. Kit has even visited a few times, and each time I mention Casey's name, Aunt Sarah's face lights up. I myself can't help but think about the three special summers I spent with Dennis each time I see her or hear her name.